Poster Boy for Perfection

Tony Trilling was signing a picture as we approached the autographing table at Neiman's. His amazing hazel eyes met my stunned yet striking blue-eyed gaze.

The poster boy for perfection stared at me for like a full two seconds. I was face to chronic face with Tony Trilling, and I suddenly realized he was majorly doable.

I set down a pile of Tony Trilling's tennis camp envelopes and said, "Here's what you wanted."

"Definitely," Tony whispered.

His publicist interrupted, with this strained Cruella de Vil smile. "So many other fans are waiting. But Cher and her friends *have* signed up for your clinic."

"Cool." Tony seemed really pleased. He gripped my hand in both of his, which were way powerful. "So then, I'll see you in a couple of weeks, right?" he said.

Clueless™ Books

CLUELESS™ • A novel by H. B. Gilmour based on the film written and directed by Amy Heckerling

CHER'S GUIDE TO . . . WHATEVER • H. B. Gilmour

CHER NEGOTIATES NEW YORK • Jennifer Baker

AN AMERICAN BETTY IN PARIS • Randi Reisfeld

ACHIEVING PERSONAL PERFECTION • H. B. Gilmour

CHER'S FURIOUSLY FIT WORKOUT • Randi Reisfeld

FRIEND OR FAUX • H. B. Gilmour

CHER GOES ENVIRO-MENTAL • Randi Reisfeld

BALDWIN FROM ANOTHER PLANET • H. B. Gilmour

TOO HOTTIE TO HANDLE • Randi Reisfeld

CHER AND CHER ALIKE • H. B. Gilmour

TRUE BLUE HAWAII • Randi Reisfeld

ROMANTICALLY CORRECT • H. B. Gilmour

Available from ARCHWAY Paperbacks

CLUELESS™

Romantically Correct ♡

H.B. Gilmour

AN ARCHWAY PAPERBACK
Published by POCKET BOOKS
New York London Toronto Sydney Tokyo Singapore

This book is a work of fiction. Names, characters, places and incidents are products of the author's imagination or are used fictitiously. Any resemblance to actual events or locales or persons, living or dead, is entirely coincidental.

AN ARCHWAY PAPERBACK *Original*

An Archway Paperback published by
POCKET BOOKS, a division of Simon & Schuster Inc.
1230 Avenue of the Americas, New York, NY 10020

™ and Copyright © 1997 by Paramount Pictures

ISBN: 0-671-01163-4

First Archway Paperback printing November 1997

10 9 8 7 6 5 4 3 2 1

AN ARCHWAY PAPERBACK and colophon are registered trademarks of Simon & Schuster Inc.

Printed in the U.S.A.

IL: 6+

This book is dedicated to the memory of two extraordinary spirits, Florence Rosenberg and Fred Winter.

With gratitude to Yvonne Miller for her invaluable help and boundless enthusiasm. Ditto to Anne Greenberg and Amira Rubin. Thanks again to Jon Marmon for adding flava to the mix. And to Ron, Wendy, John, and, as always, Jessi, with love.

Chapter 1

Attitude is everything. I mean, you can be all, yuck, homework reeks. Or you can turn a drab study session into a gala bonding fiesta. All you need is a cheerful milieu—like my spacious, pastel-accented room; a tray of low-cal treats—veggie chips, melon balls, or anything air-popped works; and your best buds surrounding and supporting you. Of course, it helps if one of them happens to be a total brainer who owes you big time for fixing her up with the full-out boy-toy of her dreams. Then it's like, crack those books and party!

Which is just what we, the best and the brightest Bettys of Bronson Alcott High, were doing this one evening at the sumptuous Beverly Hills casa I share with Daddy, a totally prominent attorney. It was a cram session like any other. Gwen Stefani, Tony Braxton, and Alanis Morissette provided the CD sounds, while the Spice Girls rocked on MTV. Bowls of popcorn and nonfat pretzels, bottles of diet drinks and designer spring water, fruits real and rolled were scattered among magazines, lip liners, eye pencils, masques, moisturizers, and alpha hydroxy cremes that renew firmness and elasticity while they protect skin with potent antioxidants.

"Okay, so who is Dimitri Mendeleyev?" Although the question was asked cautiously, the effort actually cracked a portion of Janet Hong's strawberry face masque. Instinctively I reached forward to repair it.

An Asian-American princess and first-class babe, Janet is to science what my best friend, Dionne, is to shopping and our childhood associate, Amber, is to tastelessness—an expert. Some time ago I noticed a shy flirtation brewing between Janet and Alcott's algebra virtuoso, Ringo Farbstein. I stoked the embers of their timid passion until it flamed into a fully happening relationship. A kind of Camelot of dweebs. Janet and Ringo were more than an item now. They were a left brain consortium. Between them, they knew the answers to every science and math question known to high-school-aged man. And best of all, they were in love.

"How can I thank you, Cher?" Janet once asked me.

"Give our science grades a boost the way Cher did your love life," Amber had blurted out. And Janet did, drilling us tirelessly before class quizzes, reviewing our take-home tests, and when necessary, generously revising our homework. Now here she was, stretched out on the cream-and-pink chaise longue in my room, munching veggie chips and preparing us for tomorrow's class.

"Dimitri Mendeleyev?" I mused, wetting my finger with Maxfield's private-label bottled water and touching up Janet's facial flaw.

"Isn't he responsible for the pink satin clutch bag with floral trim that helps carry off spring's most romantic look?" Recklessly ignoring the ice blue replenishing masque drying on her classic café-au-lait face, De responded from my bed, where she was sitting cross-legged in this dope unitard, leafing through the new *Elle*.

"Not even!" Amber glanced up from polishing her nails. The swamp green shade she'd chosen was iridescent and as stylish as toxic waste. "You're thinking of Daniel Swarovski, the handbag king," she informed De.

"He*llo*. We were so not talking about fashion," I protested.

"Well, duh," Amber shot back. *"We* were."

Janet flipped back her glossy, raven locks. "Mendeleyev," she patiently explained, "created the periodic table, arranging elements in order of their atomic weight."

"Oh, *that* Mendeleyev," said De, who is waif slender with way decent doe eyes. Her abundant dark tresses were currently twisted into this wicked splintered top knot in homage to Tyra Banks. "Speaking of atomic weight," she added, "is anyone holding chocolate? Every time I think of this quiz, my blood sugar plummets."

Every Monday morning our science teacher, Mr. Yohan, threw a pop quiz. It was oral, but so is gum surgery. And along with two major written tests, it counted toward our final grade. "You'll totally ace it," Janet promised. "It's way doable. The only element we need to focus on for tomorrow is sulphur. I confirmed with a junior who had Mr. Yohan last year. We're just going to do this lame experiment where you boil an egg—"

"Excuse me, where *who* boils an egg?" Amber, her face greased with replenishing emollients, looked panicked.

"It's majorly easy. It's just like to show how sulphur separates out of the yolk," Janet explained. "You see this little gray ring—"

"I need something chocolate." De threw down her magazine. "It doesn't even have to be Godiva," she wailed. "I mean, I tried to boil an egg once. It was disastrous."

I nodded in compassionate solidarity with my crew. "Tell me about it," I said, adjusting the pale yellow headband that prevented strands of my long, blond hair from sticking to my oatmeal facial masque. "It exploded, right?"

"And furiously charred the new trompe l'oeil fresco on our ceiling," De confirmed.

"And let out this ripe stench!" Amber fluttered her bilious nails and shuddered, remembering.

"You guys are bugging way prematurely." Janet's consoling smile caused a rift the size of the San Andreas Fault to form in her masque. She stood up and brushed veggie chip crumbs from her Anna Sui miniskirted lap. "Are you forgetting? I'll be there tomorrow to guide you every step of the way."

With gratitude and relief, Amber, De, and I applauded our indispensable homey. Our heartfelt acclamation almost obscured the sound of a cell phone ringing. Everyone scrambled to their Motorolas. "It's for me," Janet announced, splintering her masque with a grin. "It's Ringo."

"Hiiii, Rin-go," we all called out.

"He just got back from CPK, where he was tutoring some of the Crew cuties for tomorrow's quiz," Janet confided.

CPK, for the uninitiated, is California Pizza Kitchen, which features witty designer pies and def salads. It's conveniently located in the Beverly Center and is the pit stop of choice for refueling between shopping laps. The

Crew—including De's main boo, Murray; his best friend, Sean; Amber's third-grade crush, Jesse; and other known Baldwins—are our alleged male counterparts. Collectively they form the only decent dating pool from which to draw acceptable escorts for festive events. They are known hotties, whose parents and stepparents live in lavish estates in the geographically correct canyons and hills of Beverly. And though basically I find high school boys furiously immature and suitable primarily for panic dating, I will say the Crew are unanimously tasty in the looks division. They build on solid genetic material with excellent haircuts and chronic attire. Janet's beloved, Ringo, is the sole dweeb among them. Yet he is a full-out do-gooder pussycat who gives generously to the science-impaired.

Janet was cellularly involved with her honey, so I turned to De. "As long as I have my flip phone handy, do you still crave chocolate?" I queried.

"I do," Amber replied, turning from my dressing table with a vinyl squeak. "Tell Lucy to whip up a batch of brownies."

"I'll *ask* her," I replied, punching in the kitchen extension digits. "I never order Lucy around," I said of our housekeeper. "She's very sensitive."

"Oh, right. And *I'm* ensembly impaired," Amber retorted sarcastically.

Out of the mouths of those who *wish* they were babes! De and I glanced at each other, stunned. At that very moment the fashion disaster formerly known as Amber was draped in this pearlized plastic outfit. Her bottle-bright red hair was bunched into multiple ponytails, each bound with an iridescent scrunchie. She looked like a shower cap someone's Doberman had attacked. "Hel*lo*, I was *kidding*," she added harshly.

Just then Lucy answered the phone with an aggrieved "Yeah?" Lucy can be so negative. I try, by example, to encourage her to be more upbeat.

"Oh, hi, Lucy," I said, my voice all light-hearted and cheery. "We were wondering if you'd bake some of your choice brownies for us? Nobody does luscious like you, Luce." I signaled De and Amber, and they started going, "Oh, please, Lucy. Pretty please. You make the best brownies ever!"

"See?" I said jauntily.

"Forget it," Lucy said. "I just finished cleaning the kitchen."

I surveyed my bigs. Janet was oblivious, all curled up on the chaise, cooing to Ringo, but De and Amber were staring at me expectantly. "Lucy, you know that excellent silk scarf Grandma Rachel gave me?" I asked. "I was just thinking how wicked it would look on you."

Grandma Rachel, whom everyone calls Ray, is my mother's mom. Is or was. I mean, Mom, a celebrated disco babe and do-gooder, died when I was just a baby, so I actually never knew her. But Grandma is alive and well in this posh retirement community in Laguna Beach, where she forces heavy food and unsolicited advice on her frail and aging neighbors. She likes to keep busy helping others—whether they need it or not, Daddy says.

After considering my offer for a moment, Lucy went, "Okay. Have the scarf ready in fifteen minutes."

"Thanks, Luce," I replied. "You're a total angel!" Then, slipping my cellular back into the pocket of my denim hipster pants by Helmut Lang, I headed for the bureau in which said scarf was tucked away. The fringed silk mantle had been draped around Grandma's neck the night of this star-studded charity gala at the Hollywood Bowl.

I had chosen a classic cashmere camisole by TSE for the event. It was all slinky and sleeveless. Grandma wigged when she saw it. "What is that, an undershirt? This is how you go out in public?" she'd demanded, whipping off the scarf and tossing it over my shoulders. "Here!" she announced. "Better you should look decent than I should stay warm."

I tried to give it back, but she was all, *not even*. Arguing with Grandma, who starts wheezing, turning blue, and clutching her heart when she doesn't get her way, is like getting into a medical drama that makes *ER* look like *Barney*. So I had to keep it.

"Out of the way, Cher! Quick!" Amber was waving her sludge-tinted juliettes at me. "You're blocking the TV. Look! It's Tony Trilling!"

Tony Trilling? My knees, regularly enhanced through stretching and weight training, went furiously weak. My aerobically fortified heart pounded like the Malibu surf. I glanced at the screen and brutally caught my breath. Tony Trilling, the hottest hunk in tennis, the total prince of the pro tour, was doing a cameo appearance in some new music video. And suddenly De and Amber were shrieking like backup singers, going, "Ooo, do you believe it? Oh, it's Tony! Uh, I'm plotzing!"

Who could blame them? Tony's sunstreaked, shoulder-length locks were tucked inside his signature bandanna. His single diamond earring caught the light and violently sparkled as he rocked to the beat. He was playing air guitar on his distinctive, oversize black-and-silver racquet. The bad boy of the courts shimmered in Gore-Tex warmup pants and this outstanding striped polo shirt that showcased perfect pecs, washboard abs, and biceps as big as his endorsement checks.

I joined my buds in a piercing scream.

"Hand me my Web shades," Amber cried. "I am blinded by the light!"

"He *is* a dazzling Baldwin," I enthused.

"The best thing to happen to athletics since Ms. Diemer sprained her ankle sliding into third," Amber added. "I was, however, referring to Tony's ear stud. How many carats *is* that glittering trinket?"

"Five!" De practically screeched. "Diane Sawyer asked him about it in this excellent interview that Murray and I caught. It was so informative. I had no idea Tony owned nine vintage vehicles, including a Lamborghini Diablo."

Janet clicked off cellular and cocked her head at the screen just as Tony's musical moment ended and these scraggly slackers, whose video he'd elevated, started bouncing around like boneheads. "Tscha, that looked just like Tony Trilling," she said. "Is he props or what?"

"Been there, done that." Amber feigned a yawn. "Oh, I'm sorry, Janet. You were busy with Ringo. Maybe someday I'll have a boyfriend who is sooooo amusing that I won't mind missing one of television's totally classic moments."

"That *was* Tony Trilling," I told Janet. "In a music video! He's everywhere. He won the Australian Open in January. *Vogue* did this 'people are talking about' feature on him. He's got a line of tennis togs coming out. And the boy is only seventeen," I added, shaking out Grandma's scarf and refolding it neatly for Lucy, "which is profoundly youthful for a star of Tony's magnitude. They threw him this major birthday bash at the Sports Café in New York. I saw it on MTV."

"Seventeen? Not even!" De was shocked. "You're saying that Tony Trilling is younger than baseball's awesomely adorable Derek Jeter, who has done more for pinstripes than Giorgio Armani and Ermenegildo Zegna combined?"

"Whatever." Amber's green-tipped fingers made the *W* sign. "I mean, Derek is a furious babe with eons of earning potential before him, but so is Tiger Woods, who is to golf what Hootie was to the Blowfish."

"Yet neither of them is a Tony Trilling," Janet reminded us. "He is soooo cute!" And we all started going, "Toe-knee! Toe-knee!"

A pounding on the door interrupted our chant. Startled, I and my true blues spun toward the sound. "It must be Lucy," I said.

"I don't *think* so," Amber countered, with as much attitude as a girl in plastic wrap could muster. "Unless, of course, standards around here are so slipping that your housekeeper uses a mix."

Before I could respond to the slur, Daddy's confident voice, the one he uses for hurling accusations, not plea bargaining, called through the door, "What was all that hollering about?!"

"Oh, hi, Daddy." I opened the door and greeted him with a respectful buzz on the cheek.

He flinched and stepped back. "What happened to your face?" he demanded, alarmed. Daddy had been entertaining clients at Spago. As a prominent Los Angeles litigator, brunching with corporate felons is an unavoidable business chore. He was still wearing his def new deal-maker wool suit by Canali and not the Ralph-Lauren-meets-Mr.-Rogers cardigan he favors at home.

"We're just beautifying, Daddy." Heedless of my masque, I grinned at him and, proudly, possessively, brushed from his collar a flake of oatmeal that had cracked off my face.

"You crazy kids." He smiled at us. "If there's one thing this group doesn't need to worry about, it's looks. Now, smarts, that's something else. Education is the key to success."

"We are studying like mad, Daddy. Janet, in the strawberry masque, is a total grind," I explained. "And she is seriously prepping us for tomorrow's science quiz."

"I'm happy to hear it," Daddy said, "because in today's high-tech world of cyberspace and bioengineering, a C in science is utterly unacceptable."

"Oh, right, like sheep cloning is my total career path," Amber muttered.

"We all got C's last term, Mr. Horowitz," De jumped in, drowning out our affiliate's sarcastic comment, "but we have so moved on."

"It was just a starting point for grade negotiations," I hurriedly assured him. "I mean, if you get an A in science the first semester of the school year, like where is there to go, right? But with Janet's help, we are now cruising the Mensa freeway to a furious four-point-oh."

"That's very nice, helping each other like that." Daddy smiled at Janet, who shrugged modestly.

"Mr. Horowitz, I just have to say," she began, "that your daughter has given me a relationship that gives me so much that I just have so much more to give."

"She's not an English major," I told Daddy, who seemed perplexed.

"Cher, I've got bad news and good news," he said, putting an arm around my shoulder. "The bad news is I've got to fly to New York on business day after tomorrow. But I spoke to Ray today and she's agreed to stay with you while I'm away."

"Ray, as in Grandma Rachel?" I gasped. As Daddy

nodded yes, a medley of Ray moments whirled in my head. In addition to the scarf coverup, there was Grandma pinching my waist, going, "Look at you, you're skin and bones! Kate Moss, Schmaite Moss, I'll cook you a flanken and you'll eat!" Ray checking out my lace-edged Valentino, saying, "You call that a skirt? It's not even a Kleenex!" And Ray asking my style-challenged stepbrother, Josh, whether she should buy me the red plaid bathing suit with the ruffled sunskirt or the puckered yellow one with the big, blue fanny bow.

"Daddy, you can't be serious," I said. "What's the good news?"

He chuckled and mischievously mussed my hair. Which I totally hate. I ducked out from under his playful paw, mentally clawing for something to say that would change his mind. But panic had dulled my brain. I brutally wimped. "But, Daddy, she's a terrible cook" was all I could come up with.

"Who's a terrible cook?" It was Lucy, scowling with paranoia. She was carrying a tray of warm, fragrant brownies.

"Not you, Luce," I assured her as Amber elbowed past me and, oblivious to nail enamel damage, carelessly snagged the fattest square. Then Daddy helped himself to a brownie, threw me a wink, and left the room—which, for me, had turned into bum central.

Chapter 2

*L*osers!" Ms. Diemer, our sensitive gym coach, was delivering one of her classic motivational monologues.

It was first period, the morning after Daddy's good news/bad news debacle. Dionne and I, and a contingent of our female classmates, were shvitzing in the murky L.A. sunshine. In shades, sunblock, and tasteful athletic wear, we were suited up for tennis, which normally begins with everyone handing Coach Diemer a parent's or doctor's note authorizing their release from athletic endeavor.

I was still in shock over Grandma's impending visit. I had spent the night tossing and turning on my Laura Ashley two-hundred-thread-count sheets. And now, standing with my teammates on the fully groomed school courts, I felt lower than Courtney Love the day Oscar nominations were announced.

But Diemer's diss lit a fire under me. Losers? "As if!" I protested as she goose-stepped across the Har-Tru.

Ms. Diemer was arrayed in her usual faded B.A. sweat-shirt, oversize shorts, and a pair of Nikes that were slated to make a style comeback in like a decade or two. Running bitten fingernails through her random brown hair, she turned to glare at me. When it comes to tennis, any resemblance between our coach and Tony Trilling is way coincidental. Like, one, Tony doesn't have a mustache.

"Did you say something, Horowitz?" she hissed.

"This little outfit," I responded, indicating my pistachio waffle-linen tennis jumper, "is hardly the costume of a loser. It's by the same designer who did the regal sheath Princess Di wore on her moving TV tell-all. And as everyone knows, she walked away with like forty million dollars."

"Oh, sure!" Ms. Diemer got all up in my face. "You know who wore what when, but you can't rally, you can't volley, you can't serve! You know nothing about the game of tennis!"

"That is grossly unfair!" Amber objected. "I know that it's splitsville for Farrah and Tatum's dad."

"Hello, give me news, not history," Janet remarked on Lois Lame's late-breaking bulletin.

Ms. Diemer angrily gnashed her teeth, and the wormy veins on her neck started bulging. De and I grabbed each other and went, like, "Yeeuw!"

"What's that got to do with tennis?" Diemer turned on Amber.

"Well, duh." Amber raised her Giorgio shades to meet the coach's inflamed eyes. "And Tatum's ex would be *who?*"

"Oooo, I know. I know!" our somewhat spacey friend Tai volunteered, flipping back her brightly streaked hair. Tai was doing a Colors of Benetton on her locks. This week's

13

highlights were blue. "What's his name, whose brother plays tennis, too."

"MaliVai Washington?" De offered.

"No, the announcer," Tai floundered. "MacGyver."

"You mean McEnroe!" Ms. Diemer thundered. "John McEnroe, and his brother Patrick."

"Bingo!" De said, congratulating our commandant. I added polite applause.

"Enough!" Ms. Diemer roared. "Okay, let's get started. Who's got a doctor's excuse?"

About five hands went up, including Amber's. Ms. Diemer snatched the note from her hand. "Don't tell me you got another nose job," she growled, perusing the paper.

"I prefer *rhinoplasty*," Amber indignantly corrected the coach. "And, no, I did not go under the knife again, but I did have my sinuses irrigated, and I can't exert myself until they fully flush."

"Okay, sinuses, migraines, cramps, Rogaine treatment—" Diemer shuffled through the sheaf of excuses, then paused before Fabrina, who'd handed in the last note. "Rogaine is a hair replenishing treatment, isn't it?" Diemer demanded, fingering Fab's abundant auburn locks. "There's nothing wrong with your hair, Fabrina. It's got more body than Roseanne."

"It's a preventative measure," Fabrina said. "And if I perspire, it like washes out the Rogaine."

Ms. Diemer shook her head. "Any other excuses?"

"I have one from my mother," Tai said, gingerly handing the coach a Wedgwood blue envelope with cream trim. Diemer tore it open, then hurled it back at Tai. "You spelled her name wrong. Next?"

De, who was all in Versace Sport, submitted a receipt

14

from Shauna Stein, this high-end shop near the Beverly Center that features fully up-tempo designers. "This little tennis ensemble made a serious dent in my plastic," De explained, "and I am so not going to trash it and drop another bundle for dry cleaning."

For some reason, this drove Dierner over the top. She ripped De's voucher to shreds. Everyone gasped. "That's okay," De responded, trying to quell the upset. "That was just the sales slip. I still have my AmEx receipt."

"All right, ladies. Now I've got something to say!" Diemer began.

"Oh, excuse me," Amber whispered, "and that earlier barrage of abuse, she was what, channeling Don Rickles?"

"Let me clarify what I mean by losers," our wrathful coach continued. "Yes, you people have trendy clothes, fancy houses, parents who indulge your every whim "

"Has the envy fairy visited Diemer's house?" our cohort Alana queried. "I *think* so."

"But are you grateful?" Deimer demanded. "No! You take all this for granted. I've got a bunch of less advantaged kids I coach, eight- and nine-year-olds who are grateful for every minute they get to practice and play. They're eager, they're energetic, they're not worried about working up a sweat. They can't wait to play. Their racquets are falling apart. Their sneakers are worn through. The courts we use are concrete, full of cracks and faded paint. But these kids are gutsy, alive, and grateful. Which makes them winners!" she said. "Which you people are not!"

Everyone went, "Wrong!"

"Gimme a break!" Ms. Diemer waved away our objections. "If you had a grateful bone in your body, it was probably implanted by a plastic surgeon."

"Hello! I think you're being very prejudiced, Ms. Diemer," I ventured. "I mean, just because we're young, beautiful, affluent, and popular doesn't mean we're ungrateful."

"Not even." Tai backed me up.

"We are beyond grateful," De insisted. "We're relieved!"

Dionne's crushing rejoinder, as well as my own, was greeted with cries of "Kick it," and "You go, girl." We had courageously rebuffed Diemer's guilt ploy with a simple yet eloquent truth. Like, no, we weren't all depressed about being at the top end of the one percentile of angst-free teens in the world. Au contraire, we were majorly appreciative of our privileged status.

By the time we got to the science lab, everyone was like complimenting us for standing up to Ms. Diemer. Of course, they hadn't been told to drop and give her ten the way we had. But our punitive pushups were a thing of the past as we flipped through sales announcements and fashion periodicals at the back of the room.

The lab was arrayed with these Williams-Sonoma–type aluminum work counters with shallow sinks, and cute little Bunsen burners holding flasks that looked so Pottery Barn. At the last of these science stations, I was browsing a backlog of Victoria's Secret catalogs, trying to choose an alternate color for a pair of low-rise, drawstring leggings in barely there shades. I had narrowed it down to either butter or ice green, when Mr. Yohan finished up attendance and plunged into the oral quiz portion of our day.

Decked out in affordable, sweatshop copies of like J. Crew and Eddie Bauer gear, our thirty-something science teacher drew this hexagon on the blackboard. Inside it he scrawled a sixteen, an *S,* and the number thirty-two.

"Okay, class, now who can tell me what this is?" he asked, making a chalk circle around the figure. "Murray?"

Mr. Yohan called on Dionne's beloved big, who was inscribing her name on the fuselage of the paper airplane his best friend, Sean, had just tossed to him. "What is this symbol?"

Murray ceased writing and scrunched up his face in concentration. The line of fuzz above his pursed lips pleated like a Pepperidge Farm cookie packet as he studied the board.

"It's the symbol for an element," Mr. Yohan hinted, rolling up his sensibly priced sleeves.

"Kryptonite," Murray guessed.

Sean, in designer shades and this immense Hilfiger jersey, leaped up to offer his homey a congratulatory high five, but Mr. Yohan shook his head. "No, but would you care to share your process with us?" he asked. "How did seeing this letter and these numbers lead you to that conclusion?"

With the cap end of his Pentel, Murray tipped up the brim of his terry cloth tennis visor. "Well, with the *S* in the middle like that, it resembles Superman's emblem. And while I'm not all up on the Man of Steel's stats, Christopher Reeve could have been thirty-two when he played him."

"Interesting," Mr. Yohan said, making a notation in his grade book.

"But *bhhhhap!*" Amber made the sound of a quiz-show bell going off. "So wrong."

De shot her an irate hazel-eyed glare, then blew Murray a consolation kiss for trying.

"Dionne," Mr. Yohan called, eliciting an evil smirk from Amber. "Why don't you give it a try."

De stood and smoothed down her Yamaguchi backless tank dress. Appreciative whistles and catcalls broke out around the room. Murray and Sean started hurling gummy bears and crumpled paper at the offenders as De did this adorable bow.

"Okay, Dionne. Remember Mendeleyev's periodic table?" Mr. Yohan asked. "What element are we looking at?"

"Dimitri Mendeleyev, right?" De played for time, while trying to catch Janet's eye. "Not the floral purse maven, but the guy who like organized all these elements into this chart."

"He's the one," Mr. Yohan said, encouraged.

Two counters ahead of us Janet had turned in her seat and was now miming hints at De. The raven-haired science whiz cracked an imaginary egg, then held her nose.

"Albumen," De blurted out, then sensing her error, frantically backpedaled with, "Or something that starts with an *S* that's like stinky egg related."

Suddenly I recalled last night's study session. "Sulphur," I whispered.

"Like sulphur," De said. The quiz cram Janet conducted had been bitterly successful. Mr. Yohan blinked happily at De. And abruptly it all came flooding back to her. "The number sixteen above the *S*, that's how many protons are in the nucleus."

"Good. Now, Amber." Mr. Y pointed a chalky digit at our colleague who, post-P.E., had slipped into this demented ballerina fantasy of stiffly layered tangerine tulle. "What does the thirty-two represent?"

"Are you talking to me?" Amber stalled, her brown orbs frantically seeking Janet. Our tutor merely smiled encouragingly. It was enough. Amber remembered. "Like, duh," she went, "could it be the relative atomic mass?"

"Yesss!" De and I executed this limp Beverly Hills high five in honor of our homey.

"Cher." Mr. Yohan turned to me. "Pick it up from there. Why do we say relative?"

I stood. "Thank you, but shush," I quieted the whistles and shouts. Janet was beaming at me. And every fiber of my youthful being tingled with certainty as I explained, "Because it's the mass of the atom compared with the mass of the carbon."

"I am so moved!" Janet reached across the aisle to clutch Ringo's extended hand. "I'm like totally kvelling!"

Now Murray stood. "Sulphur?" He smacked his forehead. "Straight up. Sulphur is butter. It's badder than Kryptonite. Without it, there wouldn't be no baggy jeans or suds to soak 'em in."

"That's correct, Murray." Pleased, Mr. Yohan erased the notation he'd made in his class book after Murray's Kryptonite faux pas. You could tell he was upgrading De's man. "Pants and detergents could not exist without sulphur," he said. "They are made by a process that uses sulphuric acid. Ringo, tell me something else about sulphur."

Ringo Farbstein reluctantly released his honey's hand and focused his startling green orbs on the board. Gone were the wire-rimmed glasses that had once obscured the Baldwinian beauty of those eyes. Gone, too, were the polyester shirts buttoned to the neck, the cheesy plastic pencil protectors, the high-water pants and pointy shoes. Across the aisle from his brilliant boo, in classic Banana Republic linen, was the new Ringo that love and a savvy makeover had wrought. "Sulphur is a bright yellow solid," he said confidently.

It was hard to believe that this was the same nerd who had nervously confided in me: "Janet is this totally down

Betty. Plus she's a secret geek, a full-out brain who doesn't flaunt it. I wouldn't survive a gorge at the same table with her. I'd disgrace myself, probably hurl."

That was the long-ago morning when I'd removed his glasses and, whoops, crushed them beneath the heel of my strappy Manolo Blahnik sandals, grinding them into the parking lot pavement, just as Janet approached. I saw the spark of interest light her ebony eyes as she viewed, as if for the first time, Ringo Farbstein without his whack lenses. I'd insisted he join us at our reserved table in the Quad. And the rest was chemistry.

"Sulphur is one of the most reactive elements," the remade science and math prodigy was saying now, "and one of the most interesting, too, because it's vital in both building up and tearing down. For instance, and I think Murray, Sean, Jesse, and Jared can back me here—" Ringo nodded to his apprentices, who quickly wagged their heads in grateful agreement. "It can react with oxygen to create sulphur dioxide in like industrial areas. And rain containing acids from dissolved sulphur dioxide is what causes acid rain, right, Sean?"

"Word is born." Sean removed his Ray•Ban Predators and slipped them into the mesh pocket of his XL Tommy. His dark eyes squinted momentarily, then sparked with recall. "Acid rain is like the tearing-down side of sulphur, right? It viciously increases the rate of chemical deterioration of buildings and other infrastructure."

"While on the plus side," Jared, in bold Nautica stripes, interjected, "sulphur is a vital part of body-building proteins. But if like the sulphur in an egg yolk breaks down, it produces hydrogen sulfide, a poisonous gas that smells like, well, rotten eggs."

"Excellent, excellent," Mr. Yohan said, making these

ecstatic little marks in his book, "which brings us full circle, back to the egg. Which we will now persuade to reveal its sulphur to us."

"That is so cute," Tai said appreciatively. "What does that mean?"

"We're just going to cook some eggs," Janet told her. "When you overboil an egg, the sulphur in it forms a gray band around the yolk."

"That is exactly right, Janet," Mr. Yohan said. "Okay, everyone, put on your safety goggles, light up your Bunsen burners, and get some water heating."

There was this little anteroom, like a mini kitchen, off the lab, with a half fridge, a microwave, Mr. Yohan's coffeemaker, and a bottled water fountain.

"Hello, I signed up for science lab, not cafeteria arts," De protested as Mr. Y nipped into his diminutive galley and returned with a carton of eggs.

"School is supposed to prepare us for real life, Mr. Yohan," Amber complained. "And in real life I am never going to have to boil an egg."

"It's unnatural," our friend Baez agreed, twisting her thumb ring, which was only one of the many exotic bands gracing her fingers. "If we were meant to boil eggs, there wouldn't be housekeepers."

Mr. Yohan sighed. "Yes, well. Everyone, come up and get an egg, now. And put it on to boil. And in a little while we'll open them and have a peek at the yolks. I think you'll find it interesting."

"Get a life, Mr. Y." Jesse, the scion of a music industry fortune, glanced up from the *Rolling Stone* he was browsing and sadly shook his head. "Bjork is interesting. Daft-Punk is interesting," he said. "A boiled egg is a boiled egg."

We trudged to the front of the class and got our eggs. Brian Fuller's was the first one done.

"Okay, come here, everyone. Let's have a look at Brian's egg," our teacher called. Brian was this incredibly fussy guy who had beaten out Amber for class president. So, of course, the gold medalist in grudge-holding rejected Mr. Yohan's invitation.

The rest of us gathered around Brian's worktable and watched our science teacher cut through the eggshell. Predictably, the yolk was sort of outlined in gray. There was a smattering of applause. Then Mr. Y started grilling the less fortunate among us, asking them to describe the chemical process that had caused this fascinating phenom. While those of us who'd already aced the oral struggled to stay awake.

I went, "Whoops, I think my egg is done!"

"Better hurry," Mr. Yohan advised. "You definitely do not want that thing to boil out and burst. It makes quite a stench."

So then everyone who could escape returned to their Bunsen burners and got all busy saving their eggs from self-destructing. Except Amber, who was at our lab table, casually leafing through my Victoria's Secret Country Collection. "Where's your egg?" I asked.

She held it aloft. "I didn't do it yet."

"Class is almost over," I reminded her.

"No problemo," she assured me, dropping the catalog, hopping off her stool, and heading for Mr. Yohan's little kitchen.

The bell rang a second later, and we all filed out, going, like, "Slammin' class, Mr. Yohan. Way enlightening. Phat demo. Science is *fun*-damental!"

"Hello, that was so boring." Clutching my twelve-pound *Vogue* spring fashion issue and the day's *L.A. Times* to her tangerine bodice, Amber elbowed her way through the corridor crowd. "Let's hit the joe bar for a wake-up cappuccino," she proposed, pushing open the doors to the sunswept, landscaped world of the Quad.

Transferring the reading material to her free hand, she took Janet's arm. I laced mine through De's, and the four of us descended the steps, waving, blowing kisses, pausing for fast autographs and picture ops with fans.

"We majorly aced that quiz," De said, signing her name with a flourish on a lovesick geek's algebra syllabus.

"And pulled valuable extra credits in the egg-boiling event," I pointed out, scrawling a quick *Cher* on the back of this ninth-grader's cK tee.

"What happened to your egg, Amber?" Janet queried, posing between two zit-ridden Barneys who'd shoved a Polaroid camera into Amber's free hand and hurried to their idol's side.

Rolling her eyes impatiently, Amber pointed the lens in their general direction. "I put it in the microwave and hit ten. It should be ready any minute now," she replied, and clicked the shutter.

There was this shattering explosion. Amber glanced suspiciously at the Polaroid camera, but the glass-splintering, earsplitting boom had come from the building behind us. Black and yellow smoke poured from one of the classroom windows, carrying with it a robust stench.

Ryder Hubbard, skateboard slacker and our friend Tai's occasional companion, blew past us on his board, shouting, "Wow, dudes, that blast threw me into a fierce ollie!"

"What happened?" De demanded.

Ryder jumped his board onto a pathside bench and did an impressive slide. "The science lab blew!" he hollered over his shoulder.

"It was Amber's egg," Janet ventured.

"Not even!" Amber objected as Ryder hurled himself into a hibiscus bush.

"It must have exploded in the microwave," Janet mused.

The sound of sirens soon drowned out Amber's protest. We were nearly knocked over by kids charging past us. "Maybe my math paper is burning!" one of them was yelling. "I hope it's the attendance records!" another shouted optimistically. The front doors of the school flew open. Two boys staggered out of the smoke. They were lugging a huge carton down the steps. "Midterm tests here. Get your midterms now," they called. They were promptly swamped by students waving cash and credit cards.

Murray and Sean, blue nylon tennis bags slung over their shoulders, hurried past us.

"Murray, where are you going?" De demanded.

"We gonna volley some lobs," Sean called, "mix it up on the clay, be power-driving aces from the baseline."

"That's tennis talk," Murray explained helpfully, turning the brim of his terry-cloth visor around to the back. "It's a muscular, manly kind of game."

"Manly?" De's hands flew to her hips, and her head started waggin', combat ready for a ritual debate with her boo. "Do the names Steffi Graf, Monica Seles, Arantxa Sanchez Vicario, Martina Hingis, or Gabriela Sabatini mean anything to you?" she challenged, hurling a world-class tennis roster at him.

Murray skidded to a stop, ready to assume dispute

24

position. But Sean, psyched to play, restrained him. "We'll get back to you," he called to De, pulling Murray away.

Suddenly a bedraggled trio reeled through the billowing black smoke. Mr. Hall, my favorite English teacher, was coughing and choking as he and our school nurse helped Mr. Yohan out of the building. The slumped science prof's formerly thick hair was brutally charred. Wisps of smoke were rising from it. His designer ripoffs had so not withstood the blast. A shoddily sewn sleeve had been ripped from his plaid shirt, and his khakis were torn at the knee.

Amber screamed.

De threw a compassionate arm over her shoulder. "It's not your fault, girlfriend. You didn't know."

"No one will hold you responsible, Amber," I hastened to assure her. "Plus you're a minor, and it's like a first offense."

Amber harshly pulled back from De and batted her hands away. "I am so not about Mr. Wizard and his smoking follicles," she asserted. "Look!" She rattled the *L.A. Times* at us. "Tony Trilling's doing a guest appearance right here in town. He's launching his new tennis apparel line."

"Tony the thrilling Trilling? Not even!" I gasped. "When?"

De grabbed the paper out of Amber's hand. "Like today," she cried. "In half an hour, at Neiman-Marcus."

"Half an hour?" Janet said. "But school's not over till three."

"Hel*lo*," said Amber, indicating the billowing fumes and student mayhem about us. "Thanks to a fast-thinking Betty who chose an alternate egg-cooking route, I think we can safely say that school is extremely dismissed!"

"It does look like they're evacuating the premises," I confirmed. A team of paramedics were lifting Mr. Yohan into an ambulance. Firefighters were charging up the steps of school, totally ignoring Mr. Lehman, our principal, who was trying to get them to wipe their boots before entering. Students were milling around excitedly, waiting for valet parking to bring their rec vehicles around front.

"But we're supposed to meet Ringo and start studying for next week's science midterm," Janet reminded us.

"Get over it," Amber said. "I mean, let's see, our choice is: studying science or getting up close and personal with the torrid hottie of tube and tennis tour. Survey says?"

"Needless Markups!" we shouted, using our pet name for the fabulous high-end store on Wilshire. "Come with us, Janet," I urged. "It's this once-in-a-lifetime moment. Of course, it is conceivable that we might run into Tony some other time and place, but not while he is at the awesome pinnacle of his fame, fortune, and studly status and we are in our loqued-out, youthful prime."

Just then Ringo approached, looking tall, rangy, and majorly jammin'. "Some stooge tried to nuke an egg in the microwave," he reported, returning his choice Oliver Peoples shades to the breast pocket of his classic shirt. "So, are we all getting together to prep for the midterm?" He threw an arm around Janet's shoulder, and she cuddled against him.

"The girls can't make it this afternoon," she said, gazing into the stunning greenness of Ringo's contact-lensed eyes.

"Oh, and I'm sure you're way devastated," Amber remarked, taking in their love-soaked stare.

De and I smiled at the snuggling duo. They were such a natural lock. "Try to live without us," I urged.

"Yes," De backed me. "It'll be rough, but I'm sure you and Ringo will find some way to get through the afternoon without us."

Janet tossed back her glossy locks and grinned. And with the last vestige of his dweebness, Ringo let out this honking laugh.

Chapter 3

*T*ony Trilling beamed down lovingly at us. Dimples dented the stubbly jawed tennis pro's proper face. A red bandanna held back his sunstreaked, shoulder-length locks. Warm, welcoming hazel eyes peered at us over the rims of these dynamite celebrity-dark glasses. And that was just the publicity poster announcing the top-seeded studmuffin's in-store appearance.

The poster was plastered all over Neiman's. There was no need to ask where the real thing could be found. We followed a horde of heated consumers to a roped-off, silver-carpeted area displaying this totally hot tennis gear.

There were racks of baggy shorts and tennis skirts in hues more electric than Amber's henna-tinted hair, form-hugging tees, crop tops, sweaters, warmup ensembles, and even structured sneakers with neon bright panels. And every irresistible item bore Tony's double-T brand in the striking black-and-silver color combo of his famous racquet. There was even a jewelry section with little tennis racquet charms, earrings, and these excellent tennis bracelets.

Tony himself was not yet available for autographs. But a queue was forming in front of the table where he was expected. "Should we, like, get in line?" De asked, her skilled fingers assessing the fabric of a sassy blue crop top emblazoned with Tony's def logo.

"Not even! We can't show up empty-handed," I said, holding these fuchsia baggy shorts in front of me and studying the look in a three-way mirror. "That would be furiously rude. Tony is here to promote his signature line, right?"

"It would be heinously unsupportive to show up at his table empty-handed," De agreed.

Amber was already hunting and gathering. Arms filled with sweats and sweaters, she announced, "Two shopping bags apiece brimming with clean gear is the least we can do to endorse this Baldwin's effort."

So we spent fifteen minutes ransacking the racks in frantic support of Tony and managed to like totally exceed our agreed-upon minimum. My gold card was practically limp with wear when a commotion of flashbulbs, shouts, and squeals announced the arrival of the main attraction.

De, Amber, and I spun toward the upheaval, straining on tiptoes to see over the heads of the crowd. Still, I caught only the merest hint of a red bandanna, the flash of a killer grin. Then all access to the tennis hunk was blocked. He and his entourage were bitterly mobbed.

"For this, I tapped out both my Mastercard and Visa?" Laden with purchases, De was distraught. "We'll never get to see Tony. Where did all these randoms come from?"

"The spawning ground of stooges, Venice or the Valley," I said, so not thrilled by the whack turn of events.

"And none of them has as many shopping bags as we do." Amber was outraged. "We totally deserve to be at the front of the line."

It did seem egregiously unfair. Oh, here and there parcels were clutched in nervously fidgeting fingers. But they were insignificant packages that could hold a few pairs of signature sneakers with, maybe, like a tiny T-shirt thrown in. Not one of the multiple Monets waiting on that line to see Tony had truly been stoked to shop. In quality and quantity, we so ruled.

I felt I could work with that. "Do you have your receipts?" I asked my bigs while scanning the room. Tony's people were trying to organize the chaos, herding his hysterical fans into a single line that snaked around Junior Petites and Young Careers to the Siberia of Plus Sizes.

Standing off to the side, bossing around this small crew of gofers, was a twenty-something Betty in a black silk single-breasted Armani pantsuit. Her attitude and attire, even the way she had these slick, tortoiseshell sunglasses from Nikon pushed back on top of her head, told me that she was the take-charge woman I was looking for. Plus she was holding a clipboard, which is such a giveaway. "Okay, I see a person in authority," I told my buds, collecting the sheaf of receipts they'd dug out of their furry backpacks. "Follow me."

"Look at them." Amber pointed to a gaggle of practically empty-handed girls. "You call yourselves shoppers?" she demanded, jostling past them.

"Excuse me." I approached the clipboard-bearing, Armani-clad blond. "My name is Cher Horowitz." I set down my purchases and extended my hand, which I have to say looked totally golden, not just due to the refreshing, triple-action hydrating moisturizer I regularly use, but because of the fierce French tips I'd recently had installed. "And these are my friends Dionne and Amber. We are like monster fans of *Tony's* as you can see," I added, indicating our abundant acquisitions.

The woman, whose tennis racquet-shaped nametag identified her as Abigail, had an excellent handshake, all dry and firm. Her eyes checked us out with the speed of a CPA's calculator, but she was like smiling pleasantly.

"If further proof is necessary, Abby," I continued, "I offer in evidence this serious stack of receipts, which we think Tony would find way amusing to autograph."

"Cher's Dad is a totally major attorney," De interjected.

Suddenly Ambular went into pit bull mode. Seizing the handful of shopping receipts, she pushed between me and Abigail. "If you have anything to do with this fiasco," she announced, waving the vouchers, "note that collectively we have acquired more Trilling merchandise than all of Tony's other so-called fans combined. For which we should be rewarded by being whisked to the front of this lame lineup."

"Hi." De waggled her fine juliettes at Abigail and skillfully elbowed Amber out of the way. "All she means is that we've demonstrated our loyalty to Tony and his designer endeavors through raw purchasing power. And we'd really like to meet him."

Indicating the long line of anxious admirers in front of us, I added, "Like before our retirement annuities mature."

For a moment I thought that Abby would uncork on us. But although her face had clouded, she made this quick, sunny comeback. "Spenders," she mused. Studying the three of us, in all our blond, flaming auburn, and lush black-haired diversity, she went, "You are the total demographic mix we are trying to reach."

De threw me this congratulatory thumbs-up.

"If you really want to meet the man," Abby enthused, "really get to know him, let him get to know you, like really spend quality time with the champ—"

We were swaying toward her, the word "Yesss!" revving in our throats.

"Then why not sign up for the four-day tennis clinic Tony will be giving in this area?" she asked.

Hello, it was like our limo to bliss had just done a brutal U-ey and exited at bummerville. Abby handed us each a manila envelope. "There's a brochure detailing everything in there," she said, beaming. "Plus a full-color, autographed glossy of Tony."

I opened my packet and withdrew said photo. There was the boy, himself, all square jawed and stubbly faced, squinting in the sunlight. He was bandanna-less in the classic pic, and there was that hank of golden hair falling over chronic hazel orbs, which were staring straight at me. His skinny-rib T-shirt rippled with athletic cuts. And could it be an omen that Tony was wearing an exact stonewashed navy duplicate of the hot pink shorts I'd just bought? Great minds so think alike.

"Of course, if you sign up today"—Abby tapped her clipboard with a TT signature pen—"I think I could walk you up to the table and introduce you. Tony would be thrilled to meet you. He likes to really connect with the people he coaches."

"So, if we sign up for this clinic, we'd like definitely get the jump on this loser parade and be able to meet Tony today," Amber said.

"Four days with Tony Trilling," I speculated, still riveted to the raging hottie's photograph. It was like one of those tacky pictures where the eyes seem to follow you. Only there was nothing tacky about Tony. *Au contraire*. The boy was brutally tasteful.

"You'd be surprised," Abby said. "A lot can happen in four days. Especially with Tony."

De had been studying the brochure. "This is way decent," she enthused. "Tennis Camp with Tony Trilling. Murray would totally plotz. Athletically, he thinks he's all that. But I bet with a little help from Tony, I could so destroy him in doubles."

"He's a terrific coach and, of course, one of today's most popular athletes," Abby said, "so there aren't too many spots left for the clinic. Maybe . . . let's see?" She consulted her clipboard, then blinked at us. "Gosh, just three left. Isn't that a coincidence?"

"Coincidence? I think not," Amber complained. "It's a disaster. You mean we have to decide right this minute or risk being shut out of the deal?"

"And meeting Tony today," De added, "up close and personal?"

Just then the line of fans parted and a preteen in baggy jeans and a hooded sweatshirt with a racquet-shaped nametag pinned onto it came running over to Abby. "I gotta go get Tony some juice," he said breathlessly. "And he wants more brochures and publicity pictures."

"Okay," Abby said, dismissing the boy, "I'll bring them over to him myself." She turned back to us and shrugged her shoulders. "I guess some other fans are interested in doing that clinic. Excuse me," she said, reaching for the envelopes she'd given us. "If you're finished with these, I'll rush them over to Tony."

I saw the angst of decision-making overtake my homeys. De began to nibble on her lip. Amber's green juliettes drummed a tattoo on the brochure she was clutching. I myself was way in favor of spending four days having my stroke improved by the totally hottest thing to happen to tennis since Brooke Shields bagged Andre Agassi. But how was I going to practice lobs with Tony without having my hair go limp or like getting all sweaty? Plus, of the four dates set aside for the clinic, two of them were school days, which meant I'd need to have a difficult discussion with Daddy.

"Okay, let's recap the game plan here," Amber suddenly insisted. "If we signed up now, we definitely get to see Tony today?"

Abby nodded.

"And like since you're bringing him a bunch of envelopes right now," De added, "we could like just go with you."

"Well, first you've got to read this contract," Abby responded. "Then you can sign and I'll need a deposit."

"Daddy loves tennis," I said, my hand reaching instinctively for the Vuitton credit card holder inside my teddy-bear backpack, "so he'd never begrudge me the chance to be coached by a world class player like Tony."

Tearing three contracts from her clipboard and handing them to us, Abby went, "Sign here. And here. This is a disclaimer. This is a standard clause. And I'll need half down, nonrefundable."

Like a consumer drill team, we whipped out our over-worked credit cards and handed them over. It was so worth it. The minute the negotiation was concluded, Abby scooped up an armful of manila envelopes just like the ones she'd given us. "Hang on to these for me, will you?" she said, unloading them into my arms—which normally would have been such an As if!, but today was a golden op—and we followed her through the rabidly stoked crowd directly to the head of the line.

Tony was signing a picture as we approached the autographing table. He looked up. Those amazing hazel eyes that I'd seen only at a distance brushed by my face like a warm, soft breeze. Then stopped. And blinked. And returned to meet my stunned yet striking blue-eyed gaze.

The poster boy for perfection stared at me wordlessly for like a full two seconds. Then this slammin' grin lit his face. I had caught that look in countless 'zine images and TV ads, but never actually aimed at me. A petite shudder racked my seriously toned bod. Here I was, face to chronic face with Tony Trilling, and he was like so real, so youthful, and I suddenly realized, majorly doable.

Abby plunked our contracts down on the table next to this big pitcher of ice water. "Tony, these girls are very eager to meet you—"

"You are so much cuter than Sampras," De blurted out. "And he's not exactly chopped liver."

"Yeah," Tony said, not taking his eyes off me.

The girl who'd been next in line to see him was standing there, holding this little instant camera and, like, frowning at us. Amber went, "Hi, Tony. I'm Amber." Then she stuck her head next to his and, striking this gala pose, called, "Hey, you, depressed girl with the camera. Take our picture, quick. My father's a shrink. I can get two free therapy sessions for you or any member of your immediate family."

As the flash went off, De poked me in the back. "Say something to him," she commanded.

I set down the pile of envelopes and said, "Here's what you wanted."

"Definitely," Tony whispered.

"I'm Cher Horowitz." I extended my hand. He reached forward to shake it and knocked over the envelopes. I tried to catch them as they tumbled to the floor. Tony bent forward at the same time. With a ferocious crack, we banged heads. "Yow!" I went, grabbing my forehead.

"Oh, man, I'm sorry!" Tony cried. I so literally saw stars. Fireworks went off. Sparks flew. And whether the def light show was caused by mutual attraction or a minor concussion, I couldn't care less. I only know that he whipped off his noble bandanna, plunged it into the pitcher of ice water, then pressed it to my head.

I was vaguely aware that De was dialing EMS and Abby was urging me to sign a release form clearing Tony of responsibility for the incident, while Amber seemed to be furiously negotiating for the disposable camera.

Then Tony's voice went, "Cher, are you all right?" I opened my eyes to find those noble greenish-brown orbs pinned to me with totally touching concern.

"I'm so sorry. Are you going to be okay?" Before I could respond, he twisted up the icy bandanna and tied it around my head. "Keep this on. It should help. I wish I could do more—"

"But you can't," Abby interrupted, with this strained Cruella de Vil smile. "Not now while so many other fans are waiting. But Cher and her friends *have* signed up for your clinic."

"Cool." Tony seemed really pleased. He gripped my hand in both of his, which were way powerful and fully callused. It was so spa, like getting a pumice peel. "So then, I'll see you in a couple of weeks, right? I'll make it up to you then," he said, reluctantly releasing my hand. "I promise."

Daddy was trying to pack for his trip when I returned home. "What's that *schmata* on your head?" he barked at me. Strewn with hangers, clothing, shoes, and sundry travel supplies, his room looked like a yard sale. He was holding two suits, clearly trying to decide between them. "Is that some weird new fad, tying red rags around your head?"

Much as I longed to share my magical afternoon with Daddy, I could see that he was way in overwhelm. So I buzzed his cheek, took the suits from him, returned the glen plaid double-breasted and the big-shouldered corduroy to the closet, and pulled out this excellent three-button cotton seersucker with flattering vertical lines.

I could hear Daddy sigh behind me and settle into his leather Barcelona chair, which wheezed under his weight. Deftly organizing his carry-ons, I chatted about this and that, managing to work in the fact that I'd heard about this amazing tennis clinic Tony Trilling was giving right here in L.A. And that, although I thought maybe two of the days the clinic was being offered were technically school days, I thought the educational value of studying form and strategy with a bona fide world-class grand-slam tennis star seriously outweighed like, duh, discovering that there are fifty thousand slimy worms per acre of soil that eat like eighteen wagonloads of dirt a year or that if you cut away the skin at the end of a raw chicken foot and, using needle-nose pliers, pull on the stringlike tendons that are hanging out, you can see how toes flex.

"That's disgusting," Daddy said. "Where do you get this stuff?"

"At school," I pointed out, then continued to extoll the advantages, social as well as athletic, of doing like four days of fresh air, exercise, and total tennis domination. "Face it, Daddy," I said, rolling up six pairs of classic cotton socks and tucking them into the nylon compartment that I'd already labeled Socks and Sundry, "I can make a lot more contacts playing tennis than I can learning how to torture chickens in the musty classrooms of Bronson Alcott High, which is basically just this bus stop on the speedway to success."

By the time I placed Daddy's tickets into the eel-skin travel portfolio I'd given him last Father's Day, he had gone from "No way" to "What about that C you got in science last term?"

"Well, duh," I said, moving in to close the deal, "that's because I didn't have my support team in place last semester. I told you last night, Daddy, with the help of Janet—she was the one in the strawberry cleansing mask—and her boyfriend, Ringo—who is like a total Rain Man when it comes to left-brain matters—my grades are set to soar. We have our science midterm next Friday, and I am so destined to ace it."

"Okay," Daddy said. "You get an A on that test, you go to tennis camp. But anything under an A is unacceptable. Is that understood, young lady?"

I threw my arms around him. "You're the *best*, Daddy," I squealed, showering his beefy face with kisses.

"No matter what anyone says," a voice from the doorway finished my sentence.

Daddy and I turned toward the intruder. There, in a vintage pink Chanel suit, accessorized with kidskin gloves that clutched two overstuffed shopping bags from Canter's Delicatessen, was Grandma Ray. "So what am I, a stranger here?" she demanded. "Nobody even says hello, let alone helps me with my bags?"

"Grandma," I said, hurrying toward her with this faux grin frozen on my lips. "Let me take those, please."

She studied me through narrowed eyes that flashed slightly as they took in Tony's bandanna. "What are you, a Communist now?" she wanted to know, hanging on to her Canter's bags protectively.

"Come on now, Ray." Daddy came toward her, arms graciously outstretched. "You know how grateful I am that you could stay with Cher on such short notice."

"And why not? Who wouldn't jump at the chance?" Grandma returned my grin as best she could given the tightness of her latest face-lift. Eight thousand dollars' worth of excellent laminates gleamed at me as she reached out and pinched my cheek. "Where's the beef?" she asked, giving my flesh a playful tweak. "My little Cindy Crow's feet."

"Crawford, Grandma," I said, tugging the shopping bags out of her hands as Daddy moved in and gave her a big bear hug. "It's Cindy Crawford." I wanted to get the bags out of the way before Daddy spotted the lethal salami propped between jars of chicken soup and garlic pickles. "I'll just take these downstairs," I called as Grandma Ray pushed Daddy away, going, "Enough already, Mel. You're wrinkling my Chanel."

I speed-dialed De from the kitchen. "Break out your Reeboks and racquet, girlfriend," I told her. "We are so going to tennis camp! All I have to do is ace Yohan's midterm next week and we're there."

"Ditto for me," De hollered excitedly. "Parents are so

predictable. But so are Janet and Ringo, right? They are a dual insurance policy for scholastic success. And the totally cutest couple," she said, then slyly added, "outside of you and Tony, of course."

"How perfectly matched are we?" I agreed, opening one of the containers from Grandma's shopping bag and practically hurling. Inside it was this red cut of mystery meat that I hoped was corned beef, but could so have been tongue.

Chapter 4

*D*e and I were doing our triumphal march across campus the next morning, heading for a latte fest at the Quad. She was wearing this killer racer-back spandex tank dress in lime, while I was all into a lilac and lace thing, suggestive of the romance of simpler days. Returning the desperate waves and grateful smiles of our socially less skilled classmates, we sauntered toward the school bean bar. All of our primary homeys would be there, swapping gossip, trashing teachers, and just bonding. We could hardly wait to *Access Hollywood* them on yesterday's events.

As we approached our reserved table on the patio, Tai and Baez came rushing toward us. "Did you hear?" Baez disclosed breathlessly, "A certain sizzling tennis star is giving Amber private lessons."

De and I looked at each other. "Right," I said. "And I'm

like doing my birthday bash at Mickey D's right after having a discount facial at Looks for Less."

De rolled her eyes. "Duh, I wonder who could possibly have told them that?"

"Amber told us," Tai said as we strolled to the table and plopped down our books and backpacks.

"What are you, new?" Baez said to Tai. "They knew that. But, still, doesn't it just bust fresh?"

"Try *reeks*," De suggested as she and I circled the space to exchange limp high fives with Alana, Fabrina, and Summer, who were breakfasting on croissants and decaf.

"Excuse me, but focus your respective Armani-, Cazal-, and Bada-shaded eyes on this," I announced, referring to their designer opticals. I took Tony's red bandanna out of my fuzzy backpack. Actually, I took out the velvet case my charm bracelet came in, because that's where I had stashed the hottie's headgear. I cracked open the jewelry box and went, "Voilà!"

"Yeeww." Tai made a face. "What *is* that?"

"Get over yourself, Tai," I said. "Okay, now, think Tony. Think of his boyish, sunstreaked hair, all soaked with the exertion of destroying like Michael Chang or Thomas Muster—"

"No!" Fabrina shrieked. "His bandanna?"

"You snagged Tony Trilling's bandanna?" Summer asked.

"I didn't snag it," I responded. "He gave it to me."

"Was that before or after he promised Amber the private lesson?" Alana asked, pouring two Sweet'n Lows into her mochaccino.

Before I could reply, De went, "Speaking of the disheveled," and Amber sashayed up to the table, followed by a Barney from the stooge end of the patio.

"That was way noble of you," she told the guy, who was carrying her tray. "Just set it down here and bail." Then she turned to me. "I'll see your little bandanna and raise you this," she said, brandishing the snapshot of herself and Tony.

Geek boy tapped her shoulder, which was draped in a vintage feather boa that so complemented the tawdry rayon slip dress she was wearing. "You owe me," he alleged sullenly.

"Here, buy yourself a ticket to reality," Amber barked, dropping a coin into his outstretched hand. "Plus," she addressed the table again, "I never said *private* lesson, did I?"

Everyone went, "Excuse me? Hello! Yes, you did."

"Where's Janet?" I asked, suddenly aware that the science maven's cheery face was missing from the Betty lineup. I was greeted with more shoulder shrugs than a stretch class at S.E.T.S.

"She'll show," De said optimistically, then launched into this excellent rendition of yesterday's events.

Enthralled though I was with Dionne's narration, I found myself scanning the patio in search of our ticket to tennis camp. It was way unlike our true-blue bud to skip the A.M. catch-up session. A troubling premonition briefly chilled me, but I let it pass.

"And like the awesome hottie could totally not tear his eyes off Cher," De concluded. Everyone was all "Get out! For real? That is so frapp," when at last Janet appeared.

The table fell silent. Tai's mouth flopped open. Baez and Alana exchanged worried glances. And in a gesture of unprecedented concern, Amber stopped stuffing her face with croissant. Janet Hong, who is furiously renowned not only as a brutal Uma, but as like this major paragon of your peppy, happy, upbeat babe, looked viciously despondent.

"What's wrong?" I asked, putting a solacing arm around her cashmere-draped shoulder. "I mean, aside from that mascara which is running like mad and so wrong for your complexion—"

"It's Ringo," Janet managed to blurt through her tears. "He's gone. His parents have viciously yanked him out of Bronson Alcott."

"Not even," De said. "Like why?"

"Because they think he won't get into a decent college if he stays here," Janet responded.

"As if!" Baez was shocked. "Everyone at Bronson gets into college, even if their parents have to like endow a building or set up a scholarship fund or whatever."

"Tell that to the Farbsteins," Janet croaked bitterly. This was serious. I had never seen the sunny girl so blue and bent. "They're sending him to a private school with a rigorous science program that's supposed to totally funnel him into an eminent Ivy institution."

"But it's the middle of the semester," Alana reasoned. "Why would they decide to pull him now?"

"And what makes them think our science program isn't good enough?" De asked.

"Oh, I don't know," Janet said sarcastically. "Maybe it was because the lab exploded." She spun toward Amber. "Because someone didn't know the first thing about egg safety!"

"I resent that!" Amber reared up, tossing her boa indignantly. "You have no proof that I was involved in yesterday's tragic event. Anyway, I set the micro for like a big ten minutes. And the door blew off? I don't *think* so."

44

The class bell rang. Janet flinched at the harsh sound. "I'm not going," she declared rebelliously.

"Hello, I know you're all torn up, but how self-centered is that?" Amber demanded. "I mean, if Ringo's not in school anymore, like who's going to get us through science?"

Janet glared at her. Which I fully understood. Yet, I also saw Amber's perspective. Janet's absence would brutally transform science from a stimulating learning experience to a frantic duh fest. Plus, what the distraught brainer needed, I felt, was not to burrow into the dark tunnel of denial, but to face her fears. Okay, so the steed of science had bucked off her main boo. Janet needed to get back on that horse and ride.

"Actually, Janet," I ventured softly, "Amber has a point. And you have no idea what it costs me emotionally to even say that. We need you. The whole class needs you. Including poor Mr. Yohan, who deserves major support in his time of trial. You saw him careering through the fumes yesterday with his hair all fried. How heinous would it be if he thought we'd learned nothing from that mishap? How inadequate will he feel as a teacher and as a charred human being if we still don't get why the lab blew? You can help us understand. He needs us, Janet. And we need you."

My talk won a spirited ovation from our peers, but Janet remained inconsolable. "Without Ringo, I'm nothing," she declared.

"You wouldn't say that if you'd read *Women Who Run with the Wolves*," De advised, "and I fully intend to lend you my audio edition—"

"But right now," I interrupted, "we've got to get to class. *All* of us." Murmuring sympathetic encouragement, De and I gently but firmly led the forlorn girl across the Quad.

"This is really bad," De whispered as we dragged our still despondent bud into class.

"Julia Roberts's dating choices are bad," I said, watching Janet move listlessly up the aisle toward her lab stool. "This is a disaster. Not only are Ringo and Janet in like this grievous Leonardo DiCaprio and Claire Danes-esque plight, but we are in dire grade-dropping danger because of it."

"I don't know why Ringo's parents think Alcott's science program isn't good enough," Amber added.

"Hel*lo*, rinse your lenses and look around," said De. "Wake up and smell the sulphur."

Mr. Yohan's room reeked. Literally. It was all scorched walls and seared tables, with the stinky cheese stench of ripe egg still in the air. A few lucky students who'd recently had rhinoplasty were wearing bandages over their newly bobbed beaks. Others had clamped shut their nostrils with icky pink nose clips. Cackling like immature high school boys, Murray and Sean were spritzing aftershave at each other, Bijan vs. Brut. Summer had this aromatherapy candle going at her lab station, eucalyptus for spiritual cleansing. Other kids were heating floral potpourri in their chem flasks. Still the prevailing scent was calamity.

The lab was toast, and so were we. For up front, behind the desk where the enthusiastic Mr. Yohan normally paced while attempting to instruct and inspire us, stood that squat and rugged harbinger of doom, Ms. Diemer.

"Douse that candle, girlie," she growled at Summer. "This is science, not séance. And I am your science sub until Mr. Yohan's burns heal." Turning her formidable back on us, she strode to the blackboard to scrawl her name. Everyone stuck a finger in their mouth and did this silent "Gag me."

"That's D-I-E-M-E-R," the gym jock spelled it out for us.

"Deem-er," she pronounced, "Not dime-er and not dimmer."

"Don't we even get to vote?" Ryder asked.

"Mister." Ms. Diemer grinned malevolently. "That little ha-ha is gonna cost you." She slammed opened the textbook on Mr. Yohan's desk and ran a blunt finger down the random page. "Okay," she said after about a second. "Give me the names of two gram-positive, hydrophilic organisms—and make it snappy!"

Ryder shrugged helplessly and glanced around the room. "Yo, where's Ringo?" he whispered. Then, turning frantically to Janet, he implored, "Hey, brainy dude-ess, help me here, okay?"

But she didn't hear him. She didn't see him. Our bereaved bud was staring blindly out the window, her dark eyes glossy with tears and loss.

"Janet," Tai whispered, trying to aid and abet the hapless boardie, "what's a hyrophilic organism?"

Janet turned slowly. She glanced at Tai. And then at Ryder. And then she shrugged. "Who cares?" she said.

Chapter 5

What is this, the waiting room at the UNICEF clinic? The five of you sopping wet don't weigh as much as a corned beef." Grandma Ray entered my bedroom carrying a tray of cold cuts riddled with saturated fat and garnished with briny pickles, mayonnaise-rich potato salad, and cole slaw that could clog the cleanest of arteries.

We had gathered, *chez moi,* for an emergency session after school. Dionne and I were perched on my bed. The velvet box holding Tony's headband rested inspirationally between us. Sitting cross-legged on the pink carpeted floor, amidst a clutter of plump tapestry pillows, Tai and Baez were studying my tennis camp brochure. Amber, holding the Polaroid of Tony and herself that she'd wrested from the depressed girl at Neiman's, had commandeered the glazed chintz chaise.

My agenda was simple yet urgent. We had to get Janet back in working order before next week's midterm. Or it was adios, Tony; game, set, and match. I recalled the stroke of the trophy-winning hottie's callused palm as it caressed my alpha-hydroxy-softened hand, the flash of approval that lit his awesome hazel eyes as he appraised me. Even De agreed that the tennis babe had demo-ed big-time interest in me. Was it possible that some random parental whim on the Farbstein front would keep us apart? And like coldly crush Janet's heart and giving spirit?

As if, I thought. I just had to solve our formerly helpful homey's vicious predicament. Which was why I'd called this brain trust together. Under my guidance, we would find a way to convince Ringo's furiously misguided parents that their science prodigy truly belonged at Bronson Alcott.

"Okay, so, suggestions for dealing with the Farbsteins?" I had just announced, when Grandma Ray nudged open my door with the toe of her stiletto-heeled Gucci mules.

On the towering slingbacks that matched her faux leopard lounging pajamas, she tottered over to the bed and set down her deadly culinary cargo next to De. "Here," she said, harlequin reading glasses swinging from a gold chain around her neck, "a little something for the starving children of Beverly Hills."

"Thanks, Grandma, but we don't do red meat," I began as De folded two thick slices of pastrami into her mouth and rolled her hazel eyes in ecstasy.

"Anyway," I told Grandma, "I phoned Lucy about ten minutes ago and asked her to bring us some low-cal snacks."

"And what did she say?" Grandma Ray challenged. My buds' heads swung back and forth between us like spectators at a tennis tournament.

"Well," I confessed, "she said since you'd taken over the kitchen, she thought you should make the snacks."

"You see!" Grandma turned to the crowd, grinning gleefully. "So who knows what's best for you, me or that couch tomato downstairs?"

"I love pastrami," Tai confessed, winning a pat on the head and a hand delivered pickle from Ray.

"Her name is Lucy, Grandma," I said, "And it's couch *potato.*"

"Tomato, potato." She waved away the fine distinction. "You know who loves my cooking? Your brother, Josh—"

"He's not my brother," I quickly interjected as Amber snapped her fingers at De, ordering up a scoop of potato salad. "He's Daddy's ex-wife Gail's son by a former marriage," I reminded my grandmother, "which made him for the brief forty-five days that Daddy and Gail were wed, my extremely annoying stepbrother."

Grandma carried the little plate of potato salad over to Amber and handed it to her with a cocktail napkin and a plastic fork. Then she seized the immaterial girl's chin and turned her head from side to side, studying Amber's profile. "Who did the nose, Farber or Brucci?" she asked, naming two prominent plastic surgeons.

"Dr. Farber," Amber replied.

"Not bad," Grandma said, releasing her chin. "Such a sweetie pie, that Josh," she reminisced. "He loves my soup, my stuffed derma, my noodle pudding."

"Oooo, noodle pudding," Baez crooned. "Do you make it with like raisins or apricots? My bubbe uses dried apricots."

"Apricots? Feh." Grandma shook her head at Baez's grandmother's folly.

We were totally off goal now. Somehow the discussion had taken a whack turn, shifting from rescuing Janet to recipe swapping. Soon Grandma would whip out her mah-jongg set and the night would end with her raking in big bucks.

"Hello!" I clapped my hands. "May I have your attention please? We were discussing Ringo's parents. Let's focus on the Farbsteins, okay?"

"There's an Elroy Farbstein at my condo. A regular Casanova and crazy for me," Grandma said, loading salami and cole slaw onto a plate. "He's a nice-looking man, Elroy, but he's no spring chicken. A little old for my taste. Here," she added, pressing the plate into my hand. "Speaking of chicken, look how scrawny you are. Eat. Eat something! Your brother would eat. That's who I miss. Oh, that Josh. That's a boy with an appetite."

Fuming, I accepted the plate and demonstratively nibbled a strand of cholesterol-soaked slaw. "Mmmm, delicious, Grandma," I said. "Er, will you excuse us for a moment." I set down the dish, grabbed my cellular, and taking De's hand, tugged her off the bed and out the door with me. "Call Josh," I ordered, handing her the phone. "Get him over here now!"

My once and former stepbro was currently attending a colorful local college. Daddy hoped that Josh would grow a dorsal fin and go the corporate shark route. But his favorite prelaw student was all enviro-mental, currently attending UCLA in the hopes of bettering our world. How hanging out in fern bars, arguing third-world politics with frizzy-haired Sarahs in sandals made of recycled tire rubber, was supposed to help him accomplish this chore, I had no clue. But as far as I could tell, that was Josh's so-called life.

He was good at the arguing part. We'd been doing it since I was ten and Josh was this oh-so-worldly, Clearasil-dotted teen. Dionne had thought he was a babe even then. And it was true that the boy had not turned out badly in the looks division, except for his lame devotion to denim and an annoying tendency to mind my business.

Josh was a born rescuer. And now was as good a time as any to put his irksome habit to good use. "Tell him Grandma Ray is fully flipping everyone out. Lucy's practically postal. I'm black and blue from her pinches. Tell him whatever you have to," I coached De, "but get Josh here right away—or we won't have a minute's peace to solve Janet's grim dilemma."

De speed-dialed the boy as I stalked back into my room. "So who knows how to play mah-jongg?" Grandma was asking.

A few minutes later Dionne returned and gave me a thumbs-up. "He'll be here in twenty minutes," she reported.

"Who?" Grandma asked, frowning at Tai who was trying to figure out the mah-jongg tiles.

"Josh," I announced. "He's stopping by to see you."

Grandma reached across the mah-jongg board and grabbed one of Tai's tiles. "This one! The bam, not the crack," she said, tossing the game tile onto the board. "I thought that crazy blue streak in your hair was decorative. What is it, brain damage?" She turned to De. "My Josh is coming?"

De nodded. "He had a friend visiting him," she said to me. "I told him to bring her along."

Amber rolled her eyes. "Any friend of Josh's is . . . boring," she announced, faking a yawn.

"I'll tell you what's boring"—Grandma Ray squinted at the loose-lipped one—"that *schmata* you're wearing. They've got a window full of those slips down at Jay's Bargain Barn." She began gathering up her mah-jongg tiles. "Try gin rummy, maybe," she told Tai, "or go fish. A mah-jongg natural, you're not. Okay, have fun, everyone. I'm going to heat up a brisket and put myself together before my little Joshela gets here," she said, leaving us alone—at last.

I'm usually a monster problem solver with excellent leadership abilities. I like totally live in the solution, not the problem. When Murray's dad threatened to send him to private school unless he demonstrated his smarts, I hatched a plan to get the boy on *Teen Jeopardy* and we coached him to triumph. Now another flawed family was toying with its young. Only this time they'd acted way abruptly. Without warning or consultation, the treacherous Farbsteins had whisked Ringo away. And we were left to deal with damage control. Broken hearts, falling grades, the tarnished spirit and reputation of our school. And last but so not least, the prospect of tennis camp with Tony Trilling fading from a total lock to a heinously dim hope.

We hadn't made much headway when Tai spotted Josh's Jeep cruising up the driveway. I mean, De had suggested getting members of the Crew to talk Ringo into returning to Bronson Alcott. She'd reached Jesse, Sean, and Murray, who were hangin' at her boy-toy's opulent Bel Air manse. At first they were all like, Yo, we're too cool and busy. But after De got them to admit that they were in the pool, playing with Venom and other vintage action figures, they agreed to work on Ringo.

Amber thought we should focus on finding Janet a new honey. Despite our boos and bitter protests, she began composing personal ads designed to alert local dweebs to Janet's availability. One of her efforts opened with: "Noble young nerd seeks love-starved stooge." And that was like the most sensitive one. Tai and Baez held her down while De and I snagged her cobalt leather Hermès notebook and threatened to burn it.

Then Sean reported back that Ringo was as bummed as Janet. Switching schools had not been his idea. He was way wrecked, but his science-climbing parents were adamant. They viewed Alcott as Moe Central when it came to serious college prep.

"There's Josh and his friend," Tai informed us, peering down at the driveway through my ecru and powder pink striped Martha Stewart cut-lace curtains.

"What's his shorty look like?" De asked, snagging another slice of pastrami.

Baez was at the window. "Like a linebacker in stockbroker's garb," she responded, running her many-ringed fingers through her close-cropped peroxide pixie.

"You mean he's not with a girl?" Amber asked, retrieving her notebook and quickly tucking it into her fuzzy pink bunny backpack.

"Not unless she's into cigars, suspenders, and bow ties," Baez reported.

"Well, that could be Demi Moore," Tai ventured.

"Not even," I said, looking down now from window number two. "The hair's too long."

Wiping her fingers on a cocktail napkin and sucking pastrami seeds out of her teeth, De joined me. "Ooo, yeuww, yuck," she went as we recognized my faux bro's companion. And I went, "Ugh. It's Harry!"

Back in the Jurassic era, when Josh attended Bronson Alcott High, Harrison Gross-Martin was one of his first charity projects. Josh was just a do-gooder in training back then, and Harry was this arrogant zit-ridden outcast who clung to Josh like plaque. With most Barneys you go, well, underneath that lonely loser exterior, buried in that pale and flaccid flesh, there's like a total Tom Hanks waiting to break out. But inside Harry there was just more and meaner Harry. He was this straight-A student who'd like cover his driver's license so no one could copy from it. Plus Harrison was always against everything Josh believed in: equal rights, clean air and water, complaint rock, even spotted owls.

"What is Josh doing with a viciously snotty nouveau yuppie like Harrison?" De demanded.

"Maybe he's the victim of mind control," I said.

Amber elbowed between us and watched Josh and Harry head for the front door. "Who's the blimp in the red suspenders?" she asked.

"Harrison Gross-Martin. He went to Bronson when Josh was there," I told her.

"That name is so familiar." Amber's forehead furrowed thoughtfully, her overdrawn eyebrows meeting as if to confer.

"His dad's this gazillionaire cosmetic surgeon," De remembered.

A beeper sounded. It was Tai's. "Whoops," she said. "That's my moms. I gotta bail."

Baez checked her Tag Heuer. "Me, too," she decided. "You coming, Amber?"

"Dr. Gross-Martin," the renovation queen murmured, respectfully. "He's like the premier name in Hollywood nose bobs." She turned to Baez. "Gee, I haven't seen Josh in ages," she said. "I think I'll hang awhile."

Tai and Baez buzzed cheeks all around, then split and thundered down the stairs. They were among my many easily impressed friends who found my ex-bro easy on the eyes. You could hear them giggling and going, "Hi-ii, Josh . . . 'By-e, Josh," as they passed him in the hall. Then the front door slammed and they were Audi.

After Amber repaired her lipstick and hot-rolled her scarlet hair, she, De, and I headed down the marble staircase to the entry hall. Below us, Grandma was in bliss, big time. She had this killer grip on Josh's cheek. "So, Mr. College Boy, you can't pick up a phone once in a while?" she scolded, teasingly twisting his facial flesh.

Our knight in flannel armor managed an awkward smile. "You look great, Ray," he said, rubbing the reddened cheek she'd finally released. "Do you remember Harry? We went to school together when my mom was married to Mel. Now we're both at UCLA."

Harry nodded. Parted in the center, his slicked-back blond hair fell forward as he bobbed his head. Then Josh's pet dork extended his hand to Grandma. Ignoring it, she reached for Harrison's cheek. With stunning speed he crouched into this Brandon Lee defensive posture, his pudgy paws carving karate moves in the air between his face and Grandma's pinchers.

She laughed, then gave his hands a stinging slap. "You're also going to be a lawyer like my Josh?" she asked.

Harrison gave this *as if* snort. "I really don't think so." He chuckled. "The big money's not in law anymore, which always happens when women crowd a field. It's unbelievable how many lawyeresses you see these days. I don't think little girls even play house anymore, without insisting on prenuptial agreements."

"Hey, come on now," Josh started to object.

De and I exchanged these Can-this-chauvinist-porker-be-real? looks. And Grandma was squinting up at the big guy, trying to decide if he was dissing her beloved Josh. But Harrison totally didn't get it.

"I'm in premed," he assured us. "Medicine is where the bucks are. So, hey, hey, hey, who are these little ladies? Don't tell me that's Cher? You sure have changed."

"You haven't," De snapped.

"Dionne!" Harry's phoney double-take was coupled with this sordid imitation of delight. "When did those braces come off—and all that baby fat? Gosh, you girls make me feel old."

"Not old." Suddenly Amber shoved De and me aside like stage curtains and stepped forward for her closeup. "Merely mature," she huskily corrected Harry, batting her augmented eyelashes so hard that a sprayed-stiff lock of Grandma's hair actually stirred. "You probably don't remember me. Amber Salk," she said, extending her hand in the regal knuckles-up position, as if she expected Harry to kiss it. Which, I have to say, the bowhead almost did. He clasped her digits to his chunky chest and just stared at her, spellbound.

"I'm a monster fan of the medical sciences," Amber continued, "and a devotee of surgical enhancement."

"Amber?" Harrison murmured, still clutching her hand. "Of course I remember you. You always treated me like dirt."

"Did I know you were going to be a doctor?" Amber responded defensively. She pulled her hand from his grip and furtively wiped it on the dangling end of her boa. But her eyes never left Harry's rapt face.

At least, not until Grandma Ray elbowed her out of the way. "You look like you could put away a little brisket, Harry," Grandma announced. Stepping in front of Amber and efficiently eclipsing her, she peered up at the bulky

Barney. "Tell you the truth," she added, mischievously pinching his waist, "you look like a brisket. You're a meat eater, aren't you?"

Harry chuckled. "I'm a meat eater, all right. Dad and I go up to our ranch in Idaho every fall and bag a year's worth of game. So you see, I don't just eat meat, I kill it, dress it—"

De was aghast. "Dress it?" she hollered, outraged. "That is so sadistic!"

"Yeah, most of the deer I slaughter go for Bruno Magli," Harry said, majorly amusing himself, "although the skinnier ones look great in Calvin Klein."

"Dressing your kill means preparing it as food," Josh explained as Grandma headed for the kitchen, beckoning us to follow.

"De, you just don't understand Harrison," Amber suddenly announced. "He's got this frantically choice sense of humor."

Harry glanced down at her and grinned. Amber batted her lashes again and rewarded him with a satisfied smile. Then she tucked her arm into his and led him out of our domed entryway into the long pastel-tinted gallery lined with artwork and other priceless tchotchkes. "So after med school, you're going to go into private practice, right?" she asked in her new, breathless voice. "I mean, like you'd never become a cheap provider for some HMO, would you?" she prodded as they leisurely followed Grandma toward the kitchen.

De and I scoped the scene and turned to each other wide-eyed. Harry and Amber? It was like watching the taste-impaired leading the tact-challenged. This was a love story only Stephen King could write. He could call it *The Hurling.*

I stared at the infatuated pair, then tugged at Josh's generic flannel shirttails. "I can't believe you'd bring that bloated femme-bashing bonehead into this house," I hissed at him. "Where's your pride? Harrison Gross-Martin is against everything you, Oprah, and Michael Bolton supposedly stand for."

"One of the things I *supposedly* stand for," Josh rasped back, "is free speech. I'm not going to dump a friend because his beliefs are different from mine."

"A friend?" I croaked. "Correct me if I'm wrong, O defender of the haughty dweeb, but when both of you were at Bronson Alcott, you were among the multitude who tried to avoid that bloated bozo at any cost."

"That's harsh, Cher." Josh shook his head as if he were deeply disappointed. It was one of those looks that's supposed to send you into this major shame spiral. When that didn't work, the step-burden launched into one of his lofty diatribes about how you could disagree with someone's opinion but not their right to express it.

I rolled my eyes. My ex-sib could get on his freedom-of-speech soapbox and my one last nerve rationalizing his relationship with Harrison, but I knew it was sheer wuss compassion that bonded Josh to the virtually friendless Alcott alum. Being in no hurry to join the brisket bunch, however, De and I allowed PC Boy to present his oh-so-instructional lecture on our democratic obligations. "Anyway, Harry's not so bad," he summarized.

"Prove it," De challenged. "Name one thing that's not so bad about him."

Grandma Ray got Josh off the hook by hollering that the brisket was getting cold. But by that time I myself had come up with an answer to De's query. A former Alcott honor roll student currently doing premed at UCLA, Harrison had to be a serious science buff. Which, with Ringo gone and Janet broken, was a major not-so-bad.

As we trailed Josh toward the kitchen, I weighed our chances of snagging an A in science on our own. They were poor to pitiful. Then, controlling my gag reflex, I imagined Harry tutoring us to triumph. It wasn't a pretty sight. Still, I found myself tugging at De's lime spandex. "You know that old expression, A friend in need is a friend indeed?" I asked her. "Call me postal, girlfriend, but I have a feeling that Harrison Gross-Martin could be just such a friend to us."

"I'd rather slice earthworms," she responded, shuddering slightly. "To use an ancient yet furiously apt expression, the boy is a monster male chauvinist pig."

"A boar for sure," I agreed. "But that's the beauty of the thing," I persisted, warming to the idea of enlisting Harrison's aid. "One chauvinist helping you to conquer another—who happens to be your very own boo. De, didn't Murray say tennis was a muscular, manly game? Didn't he try to diss and dismiss us? Are you going to let Murray, Sean, and others of their ilk get away with claiming the clay as male turf? With Harry's help, we can get to tennis camp, girlfriend, where the flawless Tony T will teach you how to viciously mop the court with your beloved."

"It has a certain stylish symmetry," De decided, breaking into a radiant grin. "I like it. But how do we convert the bloated brainer from alien to ally?"

"In a word?" I said. "Amber. She is drawn to the boy like a kitchen magnet to a refrigerator. And he seems to find her a close second to brisket. We can work with that."

We slapped limp high fives and followed Josh into the kitchen. In one airy corner Harry was scrunched into the breakfast nook inhaling potted meat and a bounty of other cardiac-arresting goodies that Grandma had prepared. He was all hunched over, his chubby arm protectively encircling the plate the way it had once guarded his test papers from prying eyes. Amber was seated beside him, biting the heads off pickles.

While Grandma bustled around, Lucy, I noted, was perched on a stool at the far end of the kitchen. Chin in her hands, she was staring at some random sitcom on the pink countertop TV. The show's laugh track was raucous and full of life, but Lucy was draggin'. She'd been in this heinous slump ever since Grandma Ray arrived.

"Hey, Luce, what's up?" I called in this chirpy voice meant to cheer her. She spun around, hopped off the stool, and glared at me.

"Lucy, hi," Josh said. "I see Grandma's giving you a hand."

"I got two already," Lucy announced, and stormed past us out of the kitchen.

"That girl, she's so jealous," Grandma said. "I'm used to it. When it comes to potted meat, they're all jealous of me. No one can touch my pot roast, brisket, or even my flanken."

"Lucy's not a girl. She's a grown woman, Grandma," I protested.

Suddenly Amber leaped up from her perch beside Harry, crossed the room, and seized my wrist and De's. "Guess what Harrison's going to do?" she whispered with feverish excitement.

"Keel over with a coronary," I guessed as Grandma poured rich brown gravy over a second helping of fat-rimmed brisket slices for Harry.

"No, he's going to follow in the lucrative footsteps of his

pioneer father and become a plastic surgeon!" she announced.

"Surgeons have great hand-eye coordination and excellent wrist control," I said, pursuing my plan.

"Yes, I think I read that on a bumper sticker," De backed me up.

"It's a statistical fact that they make excellent tennis players. I bet Harry's a total killer on the courts," I confided to Amber. "And tennis, as your own psychiatrist father can attest, is this choice milieu for releasing stress brought on by skyrocketing medical liability insurance and elevated tax brackets, as well as being one of the premier networking arenas for upwardly mobile young physicians."

"Too bad you haven't kept up your game, Amber," De added, which was this vicious understatement, since our plastically renovated bud was the all-time Bronson Alcott record holder in the Bogus Excuses for Blowing Off P.E. category.

"And too bad we won't get a chance to go to tennis camp unless we find some *hugely*"—I emphasized the last word—"generous dweeb to aid us in acing our science midterm."

Momentarily dismayed, Amber studied us fretfully. Then she broke out this gaudy grin. "I'll get Harrison to do it," she declared.

De and I avoided eye contact as Amber rushed back to Harrison's cumbersome side. In less time than it took for Grandma to ply us with killer brisket, our smitten bud squealed, "Hel*lo!* Announcement! We don't have to worry about Janet anymore because Harrison's going to take Ringo's place!"

"Duh, I don't think so," De muttered. "Janet may be distraught, but she is so not desperate."

"He's going to tutor us for the science midterm," Amber rolled on. "Aren't you, Harrison?" Without looking up or ceasing to shovel beef into his already overcrowded mouth, Harry nodded his head. "Josh, tell them, isn't Harrison like a total science star, a major whiz who's already won early admission to a primo Ivy med school?"

Holding a plate onto which Grandma was heaping high-lipid calories, Josh nodded. "As I recall," he said, "Harry could chloroform, pin, and label a frog in two minutes flat."

Harry pushed back from the table and blotted his gravy-besmirched lips. "Let's see if I remember that midterm," he said, squinting thoughtfully. "Atomic weights, elements, the periodic table, permeability of cell membranes, molds, spores, food chains, amoebas, bacteria, gram positive and gram negative organisms, acid versus alkaline—" The bulkster was reciting our science curriculum to date, listing everything that would be on our test. "Am I right or am I right?" he demanded, as bloated with pride as he was with brisket.

"Tennis anyone?" Amber said.

Chapter 6

*N*ot twenty minutes later I and my buds were assembled in the den, ballistically scribbling notes while Harry unraveled the mysteries of science for us. I have to say I was relieved. Basically, I am a flawlessly confident, poised, and popular Betty, and yet this random seed of doubt had been growing inside me.

There seemed so much to do, so little time left before our midterm to snap Janet out of her comatose despair, convince Ringo's parents that Bronson Alcott was his ticket to the big science fair of life, and to like grab a spa day, get my nails and hair done, and snag a totally chronic new tennis ensemble with matching visor and/or head-band.

Like some icky vine out of *Little Shop of Horrors,* the far-flung possibility that I might blow my chance to serve, volley, and maybe even lock lips with Tony Trilling had almost caused me to choke. But now, if I could just concentrate on what beefboy had to say about bacteria, the worst was over.

Way psyched over this staining process for classifying microscopic organisms, Harrison was tossing around complex technical terms like someone was paying him by the syllable.

"You totally bring germs to life," Amber encouraged him. She kept interrupting our session with ardent little comments meant to bolster the meat loaf's already massive ego. "Amoebas meant nothing to me until now," she insisted.

"Being able to distinguish diplococci from salmonella is so going to enhance my future," I murmured to De.

The squeak of orthopedic shoes dragging across a polished parquet floor heralded Lucy's arrival. My listless housekeeper was holding my backpack in one hand and my cellular in the other. "Somebody thrilling is on the phone," she informed me.

"Could you be more specific," I urged.

"He said it, not me," Lucy responded irritably.

"Sounds like Murray or Sean," De rolled her eyes.

"Or that airwalk boardie, Ryder Hubbard," Amber guessed.

"Me," Lucy continued, "I got nothing better to do than answer your phone and clean up after your relatives. Do you know how hard it is to scrub burnt brisket dregs off a pot?"

"Scrub?" Amber was offended. "Is that like cleaning? Hello, what planet are we on? Reality check. Not even!"

De shot her a silencing squinchie, then said very lovingly to Lucy, "That brisket like totally blew."

"Look at us, Luce," I followed up supportively. But then

I realized that Harry was in the room, too. "Well, not *all* of us," I amended, "but do we look like brisket buffs? We'd rather do a bowl of your air-popped, fat-free popcorn anytime. Or those ragin' tofu brownies you used to make."

"You want some brownies?" Lucy said doubtfully.

"That would be so the bomb!" De backed me. "You are the best snack maker ever, Luce."

A small but grateful smile creased Lucy's lips. "Okay, maybe," she said, then handed me my cell phone and split.

I was prepared to confront the immature Barney who'd teased my troubled housekeeper. With a shrug to De, I shouldered my cellular and went, "Okay, whoever this is, I'm sure you're *totally* thrilling. Most guys who get off on clueless crank calls usually are, but I'm way too busy for some random tard playing ripe phone games on my FCC channel—"

"Cher?" a perplexed and vaguely familiar voice said. "Is this Cher Horowitz of Karma Drive, in Beverly Hills?"

"Er, who is this?" I cautiously asked.

"It's Tony Trilling," he replied.

"Get out. For real?" I said with this vicious lapse of sophistication. But I knew it was him. I recognized the voice. I even heard this little laugh in it and had a vivid image of those hazel eyes all sparkly and amused, a full-lipped smile dimpling his bristly cheeks. I pictured him tucking his sunstreaked hair behind his ear and tugging on his earlobe, probably the one in which his five-carat diamond stud nestled. "Oh, wow. Hi, Tony."

De's head did this *Exorcist* swivel. "Toe-knee?" she mutely mouthed. And when I nodded yes, like one of those jerky backseat dogs you see in some tourist's car circling Michael Jackson's Encino ranch, my t.b.'s Givenchy-enhanced eyes and Techno-pink lips flew open at the same time.

"So, what are you doing?" Tony asked.

"Cramming for a science midterm," I said, leaning back on the pale, plump couch, sweeping my stack-heeled Joan and Davids up under me, and hugging this brocade pillow from Odalisque. "You?"

De was trying to get Amber's attention, tugging excitedly on the feather boa around the fashion disaster's neck. Amber whirled angrily, almost strangling herself. "What!" she screeched.

"I'm backstage at Letterman, waiting for the Fugees to finish up," Tony said as De slapped a hand over Amber's mouth and whispered to her that Tony was on the phone.

"As if!" Amber responded, the moment her lips were loose. Then she narrowed her eyes at me, and I could clock her brain cranking from disbelief to simple shock. Who I was talking to, or at least how I felt about it, must have been graffitied all over me.

"I was just wondering how your head was after our cranial encounter," Tony was saying. "But I guess if you're studying, it's in pretty good shape."

"A light coat of decent concealer and you'd never even know we touched skulls," I assured him.

"I'd know we touched," Tony said softly. Then he went, "Oops, they're calling me. Gotta go. I'm doing some demos in New York and then I'll be back in L.A. for the clinic. I'll see you there, right?"

"For sure," I said.

* * *

Harrison turned out to be a decent tutor. He didn't have Janet's cheery, upbeat nature, but then neither did Janet anymore. Arriving at school the next A.M., we found the girl pitifully slumped over a heap of textbooks at our reserved table in the Quad.

"Ringo phoned me late last night," she confessed when we roused her. "I couldn't go back to sleep after that."

I was about to share the clean news that the world's number-one-seeded teen tennis hunk had buzzed me yesterday, live from New York, stimulating an adrenaline rush so vicious that I, too, had been robbed of vital zees. But compassion for our lovelorn bud brutally zipped my lips. Janet was cruelly bottoming. Her usually glossy locks were surprisingly unkempt, as if she'd gotten some bogus Jennifer Aniston 'do at a twenty-nine-ninety-five discount pruning palace. Dark rings of despair showed through the pale Borghese base she'd shmeared beneath her eyes. And her gold L'Oreal Metalico nail polish looked heinously nibbled. "He's like so unhappy," she wailed.

"We heard," I said, helping Janet to her feet, while De gathered up her books and Amber finished off the girl's barely touched, sugar-free, no-fat corn muffin. "We spoke with Murray yesterday. He told us," I commiserated, blowing kisses to a couple of fans who'd called out to me, "Buff ensemble, Cher. An Anna Sui to die for." Last night's brief cellular encounter with Tony had so elevated my mood that I'd cracked open a boutique box from the top of my closet and discovered this never-worn periwinkle cashmere crop top and hip hugger outfit purchased on sale a whole semester ago yet still classically stylish.

"Survey says the boy is way doleful," De related.

"He's frantically distressed," Janet concurred. "He

misses us. He's trying to convince his parents that Alcott's got a dope science program, but they're all, no way. They're so afraid he won't make it into a classic college."

"You mean like Cornell?" Amber asked, pausing to daintily suck muffin remains from her newly painted fingertips. Her nail enamel du jour was cobalt blue, a bitter mistake with the olive green cardigan and jungle-print sarong skirt she must have selected while sleepwalking. "I think Harrison's going to Cornell. Or maybe it's Columbia. Or like Harvard, Princeton, Yale. Whatever." Amber made the W sign with her crummy digits. "He applied way early and has already been accepted," she informed Janet as we dragged the morose moppet through the noisy school corridors. "And I don't think," she added defensively, "the fact that his father, the eminent Dr. Gross Martin the first, endowed a new wing to the school's teaching hospital has anything to do with it."

"Oh, no. No!" Suddenly Janet dug the heels of her white patent leather Prada boots into the hallway's shiny Congoleum and reached out toward a bank of sophomore lockers. De and I held her fast. "Do you see that Trekkie sticker? That used to be Ringo's locker," she wailed. "And my picture was taped inside the door, right next to the color glossy of Leonard Nimoy and the autographed portrait of Bill Gates."

My heart brutally went out to the girl. Life seemed so unfair. Here I was in chronic Anna Sui on the verge of a jammin' new relationship with a total teen prodigy while Janet's close encounter with the genius kind was being torn asunder by parental anxiety. I had little time to dwell on this, however, because Ms. Diemer was bellowing from the doorway of Mr. Yohan's lab, "Let's go, double time, move it, lift those designer-clad legs, move that overpriced footwear, last kid in gets a tardy!"

As I and my t.b.'s filed into the lab, I was struck again by how hard it was to savor my joy when one of our best and brightest was suffering. Even if we aced the midterm without Janet's help, we had to fashion a plan to release Ringo from his private-school torment and return him to his Beverly Hills crew. We had to convince the Farbsteins that Bronson Alcott had an excellent college prep science program. But how? Ms. Diemer's stint as science temp would so not impress them.

Although, I have to say, the phys. ed. führer was dressing better since she'd started subbing. Okay, her suit was a retro Soviet kind of thing, your basic no-nonsense, no-label, no-style gabardine. But at least there was no whistle swinging from the braided lanyard around her neck, no sweats, thick ribbed Adidas socks, or aging Nikes peeping beneath the modest hemline. I even thought I spotted a decorative ruffle running down the coach's sparkling white shirtfront. Of course, nothing much had altered in her attitude.

"Okay, break out those microscopes and let's smear some slides," she ordered. "Hong! Why do we stain slides and what do we stain them with?"

Janet, who was still majorly flaked, looked at her as though she had two heads. Which, in Diemer's case, would have been *way* too many. "What slides?" she asked.

I waved my arm and stood up, throwing a body block in front of the befuddled babe. "Well, duh, I guess it's 'cause so many organisms are so tiny that you can't even see them under a microscope unless you drop a glob of dye on them," I said, parroting the info Harry had deeply drilled us on last night. "Like certain organisms have an affinity for a particular dye. And, hello, could that dye we use, which is this brilliant purple hue that would totally perk up that generic gray suit of yours, be called gram stain? I think so."

De, Baez, and Tai leaped to their feet and led a deafening round of applause for me. Amber, who was busily scrawling "Mrs. Dr. Amber Gross-Martin" on her notebook, abstained. But even Ms. Diemer seemed awed. "Way to go, Horowitz. Okay, everybody, park it!" she called, motioning for us all to take our seats. "And the organisms that are made visible by the application of this stain are known as? Dionne, take a shot at it."

De stood. "They're called gram positive organisms," she recited. "And I hope we won't be viewing phagocytes today because they sound really gross. They're the total Pac-Men of bacteria, gobbling up these little flagella. Flagella are the ones with tails that kind of whip around. They're very Ralph Lauren. Kind of western, kind of polo. It's the whip thing. And then Calvin Klein is, like, this phagocyte doing designer bed linens just when you thought Ralph had cornered that market."

De received a raucous round of approving whistles and shouts. "Word!" her proud boo's voice rang out above the rest. "That's my shorty," Murray hollered.

"The sister's keepin' it real," Sean acknowledged, slapping his homey a high five.

"Sit down, Dionne," Diemer snapped.

De did, after graciously applauding back at her fans. Her cellular started ringing off the hook. Practically the whole class was phoning in congratulations. Except for Amber, of course. She had moved on from scribbling Harrison's name in her notebook to composing their wedding announcement. Beside her, Janet, all slump shouldered and slack jawed, was staring blindly at the empty stool that had once been Ringo's.

"De, we've got to do something," I said.

"Hold on a minute." De clamped her French tips over the speaker end of her Motorola. "About what? Murray's on the line," she informed me. "Happy as my man is about my science triumph, he and the Crew are profoundly slumped over the loss of Ringo. They're hurting in the homework arena now, he says. And, if they don't get help before the midterm, things could turn ugly."

"Of course," I said compassionately. "I wasn't even thinking about their deprivation. For all our sakes, De, we've got to get Ringo back. Look at Janet. Doesn't it break your heart?"

"Mega profusely," De confirmed, following my gaze to the lab table across the aisle at which Janet and Amber sat, one grievously frowning, the other moronically grinning, like those masks of drama and comedy. "You know what I don't get? If Harry the hulk could go from this school to the top, why not Ringo?"

"Bingo!" I said, snapping my fingers.

"No, *Ringo*," De corrected me.

"Listen up!" Ms. Diemer yelled. "This is how it goes. We're going to swab little samples onto our slides now, smears of pond water, dirt, saliva—"

Predictably, everyone went, "As if!" "Yeeww!" "I don't think so!"

"Then we're going to come up to the front of the room in teams of two and pour a little bit of gram stain from this flask in the laminar flow hood—" Diemer pointed to the big glass bottle tucked away in this supposedly germ-free countertop environment. "We'll look at the organisms under our microscopes before and after staining them and report on the differences. Okay, let's go, Alana and Annabelle." She signaled our bigs in the first row.

De clicked off her call. Peering across the aisle, my best bud glimpsed Amber's premature wedding doodles and rolled her eyes. "You were saying?" she asked me.

"That jungle girl's fantasy fiancé graduated from this very public school. And he's been accepted to med school at a choice Ivy League venue. For better or worse, Harry is living proof of how excellent Alcott's science program is."

Alana and Annabelle were sidling back to their seats, tremulously carrying these little glass slides of slimy water and spit as if they were handling killer viruses from the hot zone.

"Okay, Janet and Amber, you're next. Let's move it out!"

Janet blinked cluelessly. Amber stared blankly at Diemer. They looked like alien abduction victims who'd just been returned to Earth and were startled to hear their names being called. "What are we supposed to be doing?" Amber asked Janet.

"Whatever," the depressed brainer responded, sliding off her stool and starting up the aisle like Dead Dweeb Walking.

"Hot water will kill many bacteria, yeasts, and molds," Ms. Diemer was saying, "but some have an affinity for warm water and positively thrive in it. Ryder, what do we call an organism that loves water?"

"Surfer dude?" the slacker guessed.

"Hydrophilic," Janet responded automatically.

I noted this fragile spark of life with optimism. "Now all we have to do is figure out how to get Ringo's parents and

Harry together so the bulkster can convince them of Alcott's excellence," I confided to De.

Amber had not left her seat. Her hand shot up. "Ms. Diemer, I'm like devastated, but I regret that I won't be able to participate in your probably fascinating little experiment."

Diemer's eyes narrowed, and her jaw jutted out like that guy who played Patton in the movie of the same name. "Okay, let's hear it, missy," she challenged, "and this better be good."

"I'll do my best," Amber promised, plucking at a piece of loose yarn on the shoulder of her drab green cardigan. "Okay, how's this?" she began, absently toying with the thread as she composed her excuse. "If I caught your drift, Ms. Diemer, this procedure you've got in mind involves like *bacteria*. My dermatologist and I have worked way diligently to keep my skin bacteria-*free* in preparation for this awesome rejuvenating deep tissue peel I'm going to get when I turn twenty-one and my epidermis gets all saggy and wrinkled up."

"Not good enough," Diemer barked.

"Well, I could get a doctor's note," Amber added irritably. "I know this excellent premed student who is as wrapped around my little finger as this yarn." Illustrating her point, she tugged the thick thread, which rapidly unraveled her frog-hued sleeve. The detached sleeve slid down her arm. "Whoops, my bad," Amber said, staring at her bare shoulder. "According to community standards, a piece of apparel in need of repair is furiously against the dress code of public schools in the Beverly Hills ZIP. Tscha! I'll need a pass for the office, Ms. Diemer. I only hope the school seamstress is in."

As Diemer scrawled out a hall pass for Amber, De and I

mulled over the possibilities of putting Harrison in touch with the Farbsteins. We thought it would be best not to involve Janet or Ringo right away. There was always a chance that Ringo's parents might remain unmoved by Harry's case history. And we didn't want to inflict another disappointment on the distraught boy and practically comatose girl.

A procession of slide bearers had hit the gram stain flask, and it looked like De and I were next up. "Well, if we don't want to alert Ringo, then how do we get to his parents?" De asked as we headed for the bottle of brilliant violet liquid.

"There must be another route," I said, reaching under the antiseptic flow hood to grab the flask. The bottle was only half full but heavier than I'd thought. And, of course, the stopper was stuck. Some walking steroid had heinously plugged the jug and now we'd have to like wrestle it open. "I'll hold the bottle, you pull the stopper," I suggested.

Ms. Diemer was drawing bacteria shapes on the blackboard just behind us, chains, balls, rods. Harrison had reviewed the basic cluster formations with us last night. "Look, De, it's our old friend, the diplococci," I said, turning abruptly toward the board as my lab partner tugged at the flask top.

My sudden swivel popped the lid. The bottle flew open. The class bell rang. And a vivid violet tidal wave washed over Ms. Diemer's one good suit.

"We're toast," De whispered, horrified. I could barely hear her over the clanging bell, in response to which the entire class came tearing toward us. By the time Diemer turned, there was a flying wedge of volumized hair, pampered limbs, and designer ensembles separating us from her. I caught a glimpse of her startled face. It was egregiously streaked.

"I hope that stuff comes off," De murmured as I grabbed her hand and we joined the hallward stampede.

"Wake up and smell the amoebas, girlfriend," I said as we melted into the corridor chaos. "Why do you think they call it stain?"

Chapter 7

*T*hat brief phone call from Tony had fiercely buoyed my educational efforts. The memory of his warm, amused voice saying he'd see me at camp was the most excellent scholastic motivation. Every time I saw his fresh face and athletically correct bod, which was practically always, since you couldn't channel surf, flip through a 'zine, or glance at a billboard on Sunset, without encountering the bandannaed babe, it totally reinforced my urge to ace the midterm. Science had never been so seductive. The combination of Tony as carrot and Harrison as stick so drew me toward academic excellence.

You could feel it in the room, this growing certainty that victory was at hand. De, Janet, Amber, and I were gathered once more in my den. Grammy-winner Celine Dion's triumphant voice soared through Daddy's state-of-the art sound system. A strange yet sumptuous buffet graced the coffee table. Grandma's potato pancakes and prune Danish fought for space with Lucy's cinammon-dusted baked apples and Swedish meatballs. A moment ago I had looked up from my notebook and realized that I could now identify the traits and quirks of like a gazillion weird organisms.

It should have been a tubular time, an authentic it-doesn't-get-any-better-than-this moment. I had brutally applied myself to deciphering our science syllabus. I knew that gram negative organisms stained red and little gram positive microbes took the blue route. Minor tragedies like purpling Ms. Diemer aside, I was totally on track for killing Friday's midterm. Yet, despite Tony's choice phone call and my brilliant idea to snag Harrison as our temporary tutor, I was not furiously stoked.

Beside me, Amber preened possessively as Harrison put us through our paces. The boy was all into how to differentiate bacteria under a microscope. Shape and color were important. And whether they flourished in water or not. We were looking in our textbook at these organisms that were like little manic measle dots.

"Okay, tell me everything you know about salmonella," he demanded, pointing a stubby digit at De, who was munching this Lucy-made meatball.

"It's a hydrophilic bacterium," my bud announced without hesitation. "And as for its pH preference, it totally opts for alkaline solutions over acid."

She had just gotten off the phone with Brown's, who cleaned and boxed Demi's wedding dress. They'd estimated that it would be less expensive to have Ms. Diemer's suit copied and shipped from Hong Kong than to have it dry cleaned in Santa Monica. De and I felt rotten about trashing the only non-trouser ensemble anyone could ever recall the science sub wearing. We'd vowed to make it up to the coach, big time. But now my best friend was grinning, proud of her answer and of Harrison's satisfied smile.

"And when we say hydrophilic, we mean . . . ?" The size XL science whiz turned to me.

"Hydrophilic means the organism has an affinity for water," I responded. "Salmonella totally thrives in warm, moist environments. Plus, it stains red." A petite guilt tremor accosted me as I again recalled the gentian violet stain De and I had unleashed. Still the episode had left an indelible impression—on me, I mean. How could I ever forget that when you dropped a dollop of the purple liquid onto an invisible microbe, the creature would either turn red, if it was gram negative, or blue, if was gram positive. And then you could see and identify it. "When you look at salmonella under a microscope," I told Harry, "you see all these little red kind of vibrating dots oscillating all over the place."

"Excellent," Harrison pronounced. "It's a nasty little bacterium, isn't it, Janet?"

Our once effervescent pal shrugged dully, barely blinking at Harry.

"Ooo, I know, I know!" Amber, desperate over the two-second loss of Harrison's attention, was wildly waving her hand. "Salmonella can cause stomach cramps, bouts of spewing, chills, fevers, and a host of other fabulous flulike symptoms," she recited.

Glancing across the room at Janet, whom we'd managed to schlep over to my house after school and kind of prop up on the white sofa, I realized again what was tarnishing this golden moment. Call me codependent, but viewing the abject misery of a once helpful, now catatonic bud definitely put a dent in my bliss. And in my reputation.

In addition to performing choice makeovers on the style-deprived, I'm way gifted in the love arts. Janet's ongoing anguish was a bitter diss to my matchmaking and romance restoration skills.

I so wished Daddy was home. As one of L.A.'s most ferocious negotiators, Daddy would have known how to drag the Farbsteins to the bargaining table. But he was in New York on business way more urgent than my petite problems, and I needed advice now. Who was there to turn to? I didn't know anyone older, wiser, or more ruthless than Daddy.

And then Grandma Ray appeared at the door.

It was this epic movie moment, like when John Travolta or Denzel Washington show up to fix some poignant human dilemma. There was Grandma with one of Lucy's crisp aprons tied over her Lagerfeld pants suit, looking weirdly angelic and like enveloped in this strange mist. Was this a sign? Could Grandma Ray hold the key to Janet's jam? For an instant I went all goosebumpy. But Grandma was no Michael. And the mist, I soon realized, was steam coming off the vat of chicken soup she was carrying.

"Pardon me for interrupting the Annual Convention of Emaciated Teens, but a little nourishment wouldn't hurt any of you," she announced, brutally crushing my fragile intuition that she might somehow help us.

Harry hurried to help her with the huge tureen. "Even you, *tatela*," Grandma added, giving him the affectionate look she reserved for big eaters. "And you." She clucked her tongue and shook her stiffly sprayed head at Janet. "You especially need some chicken soup. Look at her," she ordered me. "You can let a friend sit there like that, drowning in aggravation, and you wouldn't lift a finger to even make her a bowl of soup?"

Before I could respond, Lucy was at the door, toting a tray of fresh baked brownies. "That girl don't need soup," she grumbled dismissively to Grandma. "Put on your pointy little glasses and take a good look at her. She's not starving. She's heartbroken. And for heartbreak, chocolate is the answer!" Shoving Grandma's platter of prune Danish dangerously close to the edge of the coffee table, Lucy set down her tray of brownies with a challenging clang.

"If you read a book once in a while or even opened a newspaper," Grandma began indignantly, barely pausing to whack Amber's hand with the soup ladle when she noticed the salivating stooge reaching for a warm brownie. "If you knew anything about nourishment," she continued, returning her attention to Lucy, "you'd know that chicken soup is penicillin for pain."

"And if you watched Leeza or Maury or even Geraldo," our irate housekeeper heatedly replied, "you'd know about chocolate and love."

"You think I don't know about love?" Grandma raved indignantly.

"Chocolate!" Lucy shouted back. "And that's my apron you're wearing."

"Sue me," Grandma suggested. We were all mesmerized by the debate. Even Janet was wide-eyed now. "Chocolate, shmocolate. Feh." Grandma waved her hand dismissively at Lucy. "Believe you me, I know all about chocolate. Elroy, my gentleman friend from my condominium, sent me a tremendous box of chocolate from—"

"Elroy?" Janet suddenly erupted in sobs, abruptly halting the discussion. We all spun toward her, except for Lucy, who grabbed her tray of treats and was stomping out of the room, and Amber, who was scampering after her, trying to retrieve the brownies.

"Elroy!" I said, snapping my fingers in sudden recognition. The full name of Grandma's admirer came back to me just as Janet wailed, "Ringo's grandfather's name is Elroy. I remember it because it's such a weird name."

"And Ringo's not a weird name?" Grandma barked back, stubbornly crossing her arms. And suddenly, this time without the soup mist, she started looking way magical to me, like a full-out genie in a choice designer knit, rising from the magic lamp on which I'd made my wish.

"Farbstein! Isn't that your Elroy's last name, Grandma?" I demanded. "Didn't you say you wondered if your friend Elroy *Farbstein* was related to Ringo?"

"Yesss!" De hollered. "She did. I remember!"

"I'm sorry," Janet sniffled. Clearly she had not followed the conversation. "Just the mention of anything related to Ringo like totally destroys me. I'm useless. I can't help you guys study for the midterm. I can't concentrate on anything. I just want him back. I want my Ringo."

"This is what you get from eating Swedish meatballs," Grandma grumbled. She brought her apron skirt to Janet's nose and ordered her to blow. Then, blotting our bud's teary face with a denim blue napkin from Ralph Lauren's home collection, she sat down beside the broken girl and force-fed her a bowl of chicken soup.

While this was under way, with predictable flack from Amber, I asked Harry to excuse us, gathered my remaining homeys, and held a quick strategy session. After which, according to plan, De phoned the car service and, a few minutes later, helped Janet down our sweeping cobblestoned driveway to the limo we'd ordered for her. Lucy hurried after them, pressing a petite sack of brownies into the soup-saturated girl's hands, while I talked Grandma into inviting Elroy to dinner—along with his son and daughter-in-law, of course.

Amber was assigned to explain the situation to Harrison, who, upon discovering that food was involved, graciously agreed to attend. Which was a really good thing because the boiled beef Grandma decided to serve viciously required a doctor on standby, even if it was just a premed student.

So the night before our science midterm, De and I did this totally golden job accessorizing the table in my spacious pastel-hued dining salon. We flanked the towering floral centerpiece I'd ordered from the Woods in Brentwood with these choice colored fragrance candles we'd chosen at the trendy Botanica Bel-Air. They were guaranteed to promote luck and love.

"Don't you worry," Grandma assured me, when I asked if she was certain Ringo's parents were coming. "I told Elroy to bring them, so they'll be here. That man will do anything I ask. He's wild about me. If he were just a little younger." She sighed wistfully.

"And his elevator went all the way to the top," Lucy grumbled from the sink, where she was cleaning veggies for the crudités.

Grandma ignored her. "Is Josh here yet?" she asked, lifting the pot lid to check on her simmering flanken. Except for the electric blue eyeshadow she'd shmeared on her lids, she looked majorly choice. Her hair, bound up in a def French twist, rivaled her taffeta lounging skirt for stiffness.

The step-drone had not yet arrived. Nor had Amber, who'd weaseled an invite to the festivities in her time-tested manner, by whining. Harrison was scheduled to pick her up on his way over.

Elroy Farbstein was the first to show up. He didn't actually look that much older than Grandma. But then neither does Stonehenge. A tall, skinny scarecrow of a man, he was elegantly decked out in a well-tailored, double-breasted Zegna with a yellow Sulka cravat tucked into his crisp blue shirt collar. What at first looked like the narrow headband of a Walkman hooked across his head turned out to be the few strands of hair he had left, which he'd swept from ear to ear, forming this stringy bridge over his gleaming, tanned skull.

"Picture him with thick floppy hair and wire-rim glasses," De whispered as, hurrying to greet her date, Grandma swished taffeta-ly across the plush carpeting of the great room, which is what we call our forty- by fifty-foot white-on-white living space.

"Tscha! It's Ringo in loose skin," I agreed.

Josh, all lean and lanky and glowing with do-gooder intentions, showed up about a minute later. I'd asked him to dress for the occasion. Which had obviously translated to fashion failure as tossing a sport coat over his flannel shirt and faded jeans. Grandma pinched his cheek. Then, picking lint off his shabby jacket, she introduced him to Elroy.

"Here's my favorite relative who's not related to me anymore," she told our dapper dinner guest. "Josh is my son-in-law's former stepchild who came in a package deal from a quickie marriage I warned Mel against, but who listens to an older person with a lifetime of experience to share?"

"Kids," Elroy said knowingly. "You can't tell them anything."

"So how're things at Command Central?" Josh quipped to De and me as the geriatric contingent moved toward the hors d'oeuvres Lucy had set down on the sideboard. My righteous former sibling disapproves of scheming. He's like all, "You just ask for what you want directly and live with the results." So don't even ask me how he's going to become a lawyer.

"We are so psyched," De reported. "And you're going to tell the Farbsteins what an incomparably awesome education the Beverly Hills public school system offers, right?"

"And clearly you costumed yourself as Jed Clampett of *The Beverly Hillbillies* for authenticity," I added as Amber swept into the living room. If Josh was a tad understated in his apparel choices, Amber was garbed for an Academy Awards blowout. Her pouf-skirted, raspberry strapless gown was a knockoff of the bizarre beaded number worn by one of last year's presenters—and heinously panned in *People's* Dressed for the Oscars special.

"Whose loqued-out wheels are those in the driveway?" the raspberry tart inquired breathlessly.

"If you mean the white Porsche," Elroy said, a cracker smeared with chopped liver poised in his hand, "it's mine."

"Not even!" Amber glanced over her shoulder at Harrison, who was lumbering through the deep pile carpeting toward us. She shot a disdainful look at the suspender-wearing science maven. "Would you believe the son of the eminent Dr. Gross-Martin drives this cheesy little compact gas-saver?" She paused to snag Elroy's canapé, downing it in a bite. "Like, hello," she added, licking her fingers, then hooking her arm through Mr. Farbstein's, "isn't conservation so last semester?"

Grandma caught the move immediately. I could see her face darken threateningly as she focused in on Amber's digits clamping the sleeve of Elroy's Zegna. Only the arrival of Ringo's parents prevented bloodshed. As Lucy led the junior Farbsteins into the room, Grandma pinched Amber's hand, tucked her own arm into Elroy's, and called out loudly, "That's them? The people who are killing my granddaughter's friend?"

Amber yelped. The startled newcomers turned to her, missing Grandma's irate question. Then Lucy, who was wearing this excellent new uniform I'd picked up for her at Uniforms 4 Us, the Gen-X clothing spot, shot them a reproachful glare and stalked out.

I don't know what I expected Ringo's folks to look like, maybe some modern version of Albert Einstein and Madame Curie, like Beck and Jodie Foster, or whatever. But they were this totally ordinary Beverly Hills couple sporting recognizable Rodeo Drive labels, major carat accessories, and coifs of the moment. A basic four-figure gold Rolex flashed from Ringo's dad's wrist as he removed his Fendi shades and extended a manicured hand to Grandma. "Jerome Farbstein," he said, "and this is my wife, Heidi."

Mrs. F. was swathed in this creamy stretch ensemble draped with ropes of pearls. When she tossed back her bountiful Chris McMillan–styled hair, a knuckle-size diamond caught the light and flashed blindingly.

It was comforting. I felt I knew these people. We could negotiate in good faith. Daddy says to get what you want from a witness or a jury, you've got to be able to put yourself in their shoes. And I could so slip into Heidi Farbstein's strappy Manolo Blahniks. I began to feel fully optimistic.

"Hi, I'm Cher," I said, stepping between Grandma and the Farbsteins, to kind of counterbalance her aggressive opener. It wasn't that I disapproved of Grandma's approach. *Au contraire*. I simply thought we could work with a good cop/bad cop strategy. Amber, De, and I could flatter and fawn over Ringo's parents, winning their confidence, while Grandma was her lethally forthright self. "Welcome to our humble estate. It is so dope that you could make it on such short notice."

"And in that slammin' skinny stretch Maska. You are totally not what we expected." De clasped Ringo's mom's hand. "Hi. I'm Dionne. Those are classic Cynthia Bach's," she said, with a nod to Mrs. F.'s jewel-encrusted earrings.

"And you look so young." Amber did her part. "Your skin is brutally flawless. You must be a frantic devotee of those rejuvenating nonsurgical face-lifts they do with like these electric cattle prod wands at the Face Place, right?"

De and I kind of cringed, but Heidi looked down her excellently resculpted nose at the blurt-mistress and went, "Elka, my aesthetician at Skin Spa, customizes a balancing program just for me. Reflexology, lymphatic drainage massage, aroma euphorics. You should try her. She's fabulous on clogged pores."

"And speaking of clogged, there's someone I'd love for you to meet," I segued neatly, pointing out Harrison, who was hovering at the sideboard, snagging hors d'oeuvres. I tried to catch his eye as he scooped a blob of sour cream onto a mini blintz and popped it into his mouth. But he was too busy food processing to notice me. "That's Harrison Gross-Martin," I continued, without the bloated boy's cooperation. "He went to Bronson Alcott High as a teen, and now he's in premed at UCLA."

"Yes, Bronson Alcott is renowned for churning out all these major scientists of the future," De followed up. "Like Harry has already been accepted for med school at a major Ivy university—"

"And not, as local gossip would have it, just because his

father, the furiously reputable plastic surgeon Dr. Jefferson Gross-Martin," Amber interrupted fervently, "donated like a gazillion dollars to build a new wing at the teaching hospital."

For a moment I could only stare at her dumbly. Which means without speaking, and has nothing to do with Jim Carrey. Was the overdressed vixen sabotaging our efforts because Harrison's wheels hadn't been props? Could she be nursing a secret grudge against Janet? Why would Amber blurt out such potentially damaging information in the middle of our pitch? And then, of course, I realized that it had nothing to do with Janet or Harrison. Amber volunteered hurtful information the way I'd always known how to pronounce Versace and De found the best mark-down at Neiman's. Because it was her nature.

"That is so not the only reason," I protested. "Is it, Josh?" I turned in frustration to the flannel-clad Boy Scout who, I have to say, came through with clashing colors.

"No, I don't think Dr. Gross-Martin's donation is the *only* reason Harry got into med school," Josh affirmed, his blue eyes sparkling mischievously.

"Well, it certainly didn't hurt," Amber insisted.

Fortunately, Lucy appeared at the entrance arch to the great room just then. "Dinner is now being served," she announced, "and don't blame me."

Conversation around the table flowed flawlessly. "Did you know that salmonella can cause these creepy flulike symptoms that'll have you blowing chunks in a hot minute?" De was saying. We'd revealed to the Farbsteins that we were all former classmates of Ringo's and like totally missed him since he'd been sent to a private academy. Then I had steered the discourse back to Harrison's acceptance at an Ivy League grad school. Harrison and Josh both gave these trippin' testimonials to the excellence of Bronson Alcott's science curriculum and how they couldn't have aced their entrance exams without it. And to prove what a down college prep program it was, De and I had started spouting all this impressive science trivia.

But now as I glanced hopefully at our guests to check out the effects on them of De's salmonella revelations, I noticed that Ringo's dad was shaking his head.

"I don't know how you kids can learn anything there," Jerome said, tossing this minimalist taupe napkin by Calvin Klein onto the table. "When Heidi and I heard that the lab had exploded because some idiot stuck an egg in the microwave, well, that was the last straw."

"Oh, and like nobody said anything about the boneheads who poured gentian violet gram stain all over our coach, who's like subbing for Mr. Yohan?" Amber demanded defensively.

"You see," said Heidi. "That's just what I mean. There's no discipline, no safety standards. Science instruction is left to a physical education teacher—"

"Hello, excuse me," I interrupted. "But Ms. Diemer, our science sub, is an extremely disciplined and capable person. In addition to her everyday science and gym chores, she runs this enriching after-school program for financially challenged tennis ingenues."

"And"—De quickly took up the torch—"both Ms. Diemer and Mr. Yohan adhere to the strictest lab safety standards, insisting that we wear protective eye gear whenever appropriate. Even if everyone starts groaning, because not only are safety goggles frantically nerdly, turning one instantly into a random Moe, but there's no way to slip an elastic band over your head without bitterly mangling your 'do. Of course, most of our class has taken a pass on the generic goggles available at the B.A. bookstore and gone straight to L.A. Eyeworks on Melrose to work out their custom goggle needs."

"Plus," I continued, "in a school that nurtures creativity and discovery, a school such as Bronson Alcott, where talented and extremely well-dressed young people are encouraged to push the envelope on experimentation, an egg is likely to shatter now and then."

I noticed that Josh was grinning. I was about to throw him an evil squinchie, when he gave me this noble thumbs-up sign, which so stoked my ego and frantically refueled my tirade. "I mean, that's why we're in school, isn't it? To make mistakes. To learn. No one grows by being cautious, do they?" I asked, pausing to search the faces of those still trying to digest Grandma's flanken.

"You go, girl," De cheered me.

"Everyone makes mistakes," Amber agreed.

"No one's horizons expand by playing it safe." I put my case before the astonished Farbsteins. "And isn't that what you're doing to Ringo? Playing it safe? Stowing him away against his wishes in some stifling, pampered institution? Stunting his creativity, his independence, his social and scientific growth? Ladies and gentlemen," I said, pushing back my chair and throwing down my Calvin napkin, "Ringo belongs at Bronson Alcott, among the friends who nurture and need him!"

There was a moment's silence. Then Elroy Farbstein said, "What's she talking about?"

"About your grandson," Grandma informed him.

"These people, sitting there, eating flanken at my table—"
She stood suddenly, pointing a grave finger at Jerome and
Heidi. "They took your Ringo—what kind of name is that
anyway? You let a child of yours name a son Ringo? They
took that boy out of public school. Now his girlfriend hangs
around this house as lively as a stuffed lox. That girl, she's
a cute girl with gorgeous black hair to die for and, from
what I hear, a brilliant mind. She's in such misery you
shouldn't know."

"Is this true?" Elroy asked his son.

"Pop, listen to me," Jerome responded.

"This is why I cashed in that annuity?" his father rolled
on. "So that you could send my grandson to some fancy
shmancy private academy? Because a public school like I
went to and you went to is suddenly not good enough for
my Ringo?

"Now, Elroy," Heidi began.

"Elroy's a beautiful name," Grandma decided, brushing
an imaginary speck of lint off Mr. Farbstein's meticulously
padded suit shoulder.

"You think so?" Mr. Farbstein said, turning with some
effort to fix Grandma with a watery yet affectionate pale
blue gaze. "So what are you doing next Saturday? They're
having a comedian from the Catskills at the condo. You'll
go to the show with me?"

"You'll tell your son to send that genius of his back to my
granddaughter's school?" Grandma asked.

"Jerome, we've got to talk," said the senior Farbstein,
pushing his chair back from the table. "Come on. Let's
take a little walk around the grounds."

Half an hour later, when everyone was back at the table
and, having finished off Lucy's most excellent brownies à la

mode ever, were washing down the meal with Maalox, De and I excused ourselves. In the privacy of the den, where Janet had yesterday slumped and Harrison prepped us for science success, we hollered, "Yesssss!" and slapped hands in a jubilant high five. Then I called Janet and De called Murray. "Ringo's coming back!" we told them.

Chapter 8

*R*yder wheeled around the science lab aisles on his Apocalypse Implosion board, collecting test papers. I held mine out, and he snagged it while executing this way flamboyant midair pivot. The slacker's skateboard move so tallied with my mood. I raised my taut, tanned arms and stretched languidly. The ribbed midriff of my hot pink, sleeveless Richard Tyler crop top rose, revealing the glint of my lucky gold faux navel ring. I felt like I was furiously soaring.

Had there been one question on the entire midterm that had brought me to a panicky squealing halt? Not even! From Mendeleyev to microbes, I brutally creamed the test. Now, setting down my pink feather–plumed pen next to the petite portrait of Tony I'd arrayed on my side of the lab table, I stared at the hottie who'd made it all possible.

I had torn the slammin', stubbly-jawed portrait out of a *Vanity Fair* profile of my soon-to-be up-close and personal tennis guru. It sat in this romantic silver frame I'd picked up at a def accessories shop near King's Road in West Hollywood, where De and I once spotted Jennifer Jason Leigh sipping latte and browsing *Spin*. In just a few days that face, those cloudless hazel eyes, would light up at the sight of me. If Tony Trilling had not been such a furiously desirable role model type babe, would I and my t.b.'s have even gone for the science gold? Duh, I guess not.

"Total A-plus!" De enthused as Ryder skidded past her side of our counter and snagged my t.b.'s midterm. "Cherissima, if I ever need an eye lift or wattle tuck, I'm definitely assigning my insurance benefits to Dr. Harrison Gross-Martin. Bless the bloated brainer. He did us a major props."

"Look over there, De," I urged my exhilarated table mate.

Across the aisle, sharing a lab counter with our fave fashion cipher, Ambu-lame, sat a new Janet—a Janet with a smile on her lips, color in her cheeks, and deep fortifying conditioners lending healthy sheen to her hair. Two rows ahead of our revitalized bud was Ringo surrounded by Murray, Jesse, Jared, Sean, and sundry grateful members of the Crew.

For the past three days, through his darkest private school hours, Ringo had heeded his homeys' desperate pleas and taken time out of his crushing schedule to tutor them. Now Murray and Jesse lifted the slender whiz kid onto their respective Nautica- and A/X-clad shoulders, while Sean hiked up his drooping baggies, turned the bill of his Kangol cap sideways, and slapped fives with everyone in sight.

Janet sighed at the sight of her soul mate being celebrated.

"Our girl is like goldenly glowing," De said.

Ms. Diemer, I realized with a stab of guilt, was also glowing, only purpley. She'd shorn her locks in a futile attempt to rid her follicles of their violet hue. The buzz cut actually looked kind of cool and punk with the swatch of color staining it. But the purple patches striping her cheek, ear, and neck were bitterly unattractive.

"Girlfriend, we've got to repair the damage we so inadvertently wreaked on Ms. Diemer," I told De. "She looks like Streako the makeup-challenged clown."

"I'm in such sync. But we don't have to tell her we were the gram stain sloshers, do we?" De queried.

"Totally not. I don't see what good that would do," I concurred. "But we should cook up some significant charitable act. Let's put it on the agenda for, say, right after . . ."

"Tennis camp!" De and I shrieked in unison.

Mr. Yohan returned on Monday, when the test results were posted. His chin and nose were bandaged. He said the surge in grades was startling and wondered whether it had anything to do with his absence. Everyone went, "Not even! We missed you! Show us your head again!"

He was wearing this Perry Ellis America cap that the Crew had given him as a get-well gift. For the third time since class began, he took off the hat and displayed the raggedy tufts of singed hair left on his skull. His head looked like a topographic map of the South Pacific, dotted with all these hairy little atolls and islands.

Ms. Diemer, too, was bitterly impressed with our amazing progress. "I underestimated you, Horowitz," she confessed when I showed up for P.E. wearing one of the vivid little tennis skirts I'd snagged at Tony's autographing. "I thought you and your pampered pals were just a bunch of spoiled losers, but you aced that science exam, and my hat's off to you."

The coach was speaking metaphorically. Unlike Yohan, there was no cap hiding her stained head. No bandages over her streaked visage. I could barely glimpse her poly-hued face without suffering pangs of remorse. "I think it's a total testament to your compassionate teaching technique," I insisted.

De had joined us and was standing right next to me. The reinforced toe of her tangerine and white Tony Trilling Grand Slam Champion footwear toyed with the tennis court clay. She would not even look up at Ms. Diemer. I tugged at my t.b.'s skirt. "Oh, I profusely agree," she responded automatically. "It's a brutal endorsement of your uniquely nurturing educational style, Ms. Diemer. And I and my cohorts are way grateful."

"Omigod, she's crying," Tai whispered behind us.

"Am not!" Ms. Diemer roared, wiping her eyes with the back of one purple-blotched hand. "I just got something in my eye, is all. Okay, let's go." She blew a shrill blast on her whistle. "Lemme have those excuses!"

It was a day of triumph and gladness. I don't know which excellent event was the second runner-up for best moment: the sight of Janet and Ringo crossing the Quad together, hands locked, eyes glassy with devotion; big Harry picking Amber up in front of the school in this loqued-out white Porsche—which we found out later the pushy vixen had talked Elroy Farbstein into lending her new boo for the occasion; or Murray and De drawing a crowd as they argued gender issues on the sunlit cafeteria patio, as in golden oldie days.

"Can I whup your booty in tennis?" Murray asked rhetorically. "As Gwen Stefani would say, No Doubt!"

"As Shirley Manson would respond," De countered, French tips curled into fists on her hips, "Garbage!"

But I do know what took top prize and second best in the moments-to-treasure sweepstakes. The first, hands down, was Daddy's viciously stoked response to my perfect test paper when he returned from New York that night. He totally beamed at me. "That's my smartie," he crooned, chucking me under the chin. Then he grabbed a piece of pastrami from the buffet Grandma had prepared for him and waggled it at me. "Now, tell me, what did you start with and how hard did you have to negotiate to bring it up from there?"

"Hello," I said, removing the cold-cut remnant from his clutches a moment before he trashed his mouth with it. "It started with an A and it ended with an A. I didn't have to negotiate anything, Daddy."

"No!" he said, stunned.

"Yes! I fiercely aced my science midterm," I proudly reported.

"I mean, no, don't grab pastrami out of my hand," Daddy said.

Second best to Daddy's joy was Grandma's leaving. I mean, I knew we couldn't have accomplished Ringo's return without her. And I was frantically grateful for her help. Plus her staying with me at our opulent L.A. mansionette took a serious stress load off Daddy's overburdened being. Still, I'd gained a solid three-quarters of a pound since she'd come and used like two whole concealer sticks trying to naturalize the red and blue marks her pinching and prodding had left on my formerly blemishless bod. So I was not like radically broken up when it came to say adieu.

Grandma was all packed and ready to shove off. Elroy had recalled his wheels from Harrison and, as twilight and substandard air conditions enflamed the sky above the hills of Beverly, was dozing in his Porsche in the driveway, waiting to take her home.

"Can I help you with that suitcase, Grandma Ray?" I offered, picking up her ancient Vuitton satchel.

"Why, I look like a cripple to you?" she responded, jerking the bag from my hand.

"No, Grandma," I acquiesced, throwing my hands in the air. "I'd just like to do something for you after all you did for me and my friends this week. I mean, you totally supported our academic efforts by keeping Harrison perpetually fed. Janet and Ringo are an educational resource again."

"Okay, tell you what," Grandma said. "Give me that test paper you just got an A on."

"You want my midterm?" I couldn't believe it.

"Absolutely," said Grandma. "I'm going to have it laminated, so it won't get wet when I show it to my friends at the condominium pool . . . and watch them go green with envy!" She cackled, then opened her arms to me. "Come on, gimme a kiss!"

I did, moving cautiously into her embrace, warily expecting a pinch or a poke at any moment. But all I got was this bone-crushing hug and Grandma's voice in my ear, going, "Your mother would be so proud of you, *mamela*. You're smart and beautiful and a do-gooder just like she was."

"Thank you, Grandma," I said.

"Only you're too skinny," she added, releasing me.

I ran back to my room and got her the test paper. On my way downstairs I saw Lucy hurrying through the entry hall with a picnic hamper in her hands. "What's that, Luce?" I inquired, waving my exam at Grandma, who was on our white-columned veranda now, waiting for me.

"I packed her some goodies for the trip," Lucy confessed.

"Oh, Luce, that is so loving of you," I commended our housekeeper on the noble conciliatory gesture. "You've seen through Grandma Ray's harsh, bossy exterior to the nurturing woman she truly is."

"Nurturing, schmurturing," said Lucy. "I'm just thrilled she's leaving!"

Tscha! The golden day dawned. Tony's tennis camp was nestled in the Santa Monica Mountains. With De at the wheel of her mom's four-by-four and me navigating with the furiously inadequate little map that had come in our orientation packet, we took the hills above Sunset a hairpin turn at a time. In the backseat, flanked by mountains of luggage, Amber was cooing cellularly to Harry.

"He's like so lost without me," she paused to inform us. Then returning to the phone, she snapped, "What do you mean you're going to a movie tonight? You know that I'm not available tonight. Of course I like Jackie Chan. She's one of my total favorites. Big deal, so he's a man. I knew that, Harrison. I meant, *he* is one of my total favorites."

"How's my hair, De?" I asked, checking my freshly highlighted and styled mane for the umpteenth time in the windshield visor mirror. It looked actually excellent, but I could only glom a frontal view. You never knew—my rear locks might be brutally bed head.

"Way better looking than Mr. Yohan's," my bud assured me with a mischievous grin. De's raven locks were adorably ponytailed, peeking out from under this chronic, floppy-brimmed crocheted hat. "I hope Tony is as fabu a tennis coach as he is a player," she added. "I really want to ego-slam Murray when we get home. He's all, women are cosmetic, not athletic. Like that's all we're into, looks and clothes."

"That is so unfair," I commiserated, scooching a finger preventatively across my top teeth, even though not a speck of Estee's stain-free, lip-soothing indelible color had strayed onto my sparkling whites.

"Profusely," De concurred. "Plus he thinks he's all that at the game."

"High school boys are so hormonal," I observed.

"Who are we trashing?" Amber asked eagerly, clicking off cellular. While De and I were casually attired in classic Hush Puppies, bootleg jeans, and ribbed knit tees, Harry's keeper had chosen a vintage Richard Simmons–era workout ensemble in neon floral.

"Murray," De replied as the portable embarrassment leaned over the front seat, adjusted the rearview mirror, and studied the gaudy makeup sampler that was her face.

Just ahead, from a rustic arch crowned with crossed tennis racquets, a simple sign announced Tony Trilling's Tennis Camp. The mere sight of his name on that humble silver-and-black beacon put my heart into fierce overdrive. "There it is! We're here!" I shrieked, startling Amber, who had just begun heaping green eyeshadow onto her already Braille lids.

We roared through the archway and sailed over a speed

bump. "Speaking of hormonal," Amber grumbled, fishing for a tissue in her lawn bag–size makeup kit. "Hello. Did I just hear the grating squeal of naive romantic expectations?"

My response was swift. "Excuse me, Ambu-lame," I shot back. "If you heard anything loud and grating, it was probably your costume." Yet I felt a pang of ickiness at the girl's Grinchesque remarks.

The intense eyeballing, the bandanna episode we'd shared at Neiman's, the Letterman phone call live from New York—was I whack to believe they were meaningful to Tony? I really didn't think so. Could a top-seeded, grand-slam Baldwin such as he find my youthful beauty, quick wit, and compassionate nature frantically fresh? Tscha, I decided, who wouldn't? False modesty is so not my family motto. Daddy totally doesn't tolerate low self-esteem.

We were proceeding through a landscaped area carved out of the surrounding wilderness. "Count them," De was saying. "Twelve tennis courts and no Ms. Diemer. Excuse me, is that a racquet-shaped swimming pool? I've died and gone to Martina heaven."

A large white painted clubhouse, just slightly smaller than our guest bungalow, seemed to be the camp's central rallying point. There were a number of players occupying the courts and another dozen visitors viewing the games or wandering to and from the clubhouse. Everyone was way Benetton, all colorfully international and ranging in age from six to Social Security.

"Hot tub on the starboard bow," Amber bellowed. "The perfect après game rehab for furiously rejuvenating over-worked muscles."

Like your mouth, I refrained from saying as De did this

pebble-splashing wheelie into a reserved parking spot in the gravel lot behind the clubhouse. We climbed out of the car and looked around for a porter.

"What, no Tony to personally greet us?" Amber said sarcastically. "Whoops, I guess the boy's got more important things to do than remember the little people who made him what he is today. I always wondered why he wore that bandanna. Could it possibly be to keep his swollen head from getting bigger?"

"CHER!"

I spun toward the courts, as did every other hearing-empowered creature within five miles. Whatever resentment I harbored toward the loose-lipped one vanished. For there, loping out of a teaching court, in tennis whites with this chronic Brooks Brothers cashmere knotted over his shoulders and a sunny Western-style bandanna capping his streaky hair, was Tony. And he was waving madly at me.

"I guess the boy hasn't forgotten *all* the little people," De ragged on Amber, whose electric pink lips were practically unhinged at the sight of the way props pro jogging in our direction.

"Hey," I greeted the hottie, waving back at him. "Slammin' site you've got here."

"Glad you like it. Speaking of slammin' sights," he said, giving me one of his killer smiles, "you're one I've been waitin' to catch. How's the skull?" He gently touched my forehead, smoothing back a fallen lock of hair. "Not a scratch left. No souvenir of our first encounter."

"Actually," I said, fishing around in my handloomed stringpurse, "I do have one." I'd asked Lucy to launder the red bandanna so, of course, she'd sent it out to be cleaned. At a cost that would have aerobically elevated Daddy's pulse if I'd been whack enough to show him the bill, I got it back, handwashed, steam pressed, and wrapped in pale pink tissue paper. "Voilà," I announced, proffering Tony's classic headrag.

He stopped my hand. "It's yours," he said. "I always meant for you to keep it."

"Hello. Excuse me!" Amber cleared her throat.

"Hey, how's it going?" Tony turned to her.

"Nice of you to notice us," she said, thrusting out a paw, which the polite hottie obligingly gripped. "It's been way too long, Tony. Since we last met, my life has awesomely altered. I'm not entirely available anymore. There's this young doctor in the picture."

"Hey, that's great," Tony said, turning to De. "And you're Dionne, right?"

"Totally," De kvelled. "And I'm majorly stoked about being here. My big is this MaliVai Washington wannabe who's gone retrograde on gender bias. The boy thinks women are second-class tennis citizens. So I need to radically upgrade my racquet skills."

"I've got four days with you. He's toast," Tony assured her. "But you, all of you," he said ominously, "are going to have to really sweat. In this game, *playing* means 'work.'"

That random remark turned out to be the total creed of Camp Tony. After we got our bags stowed away in this meager yet doable bunkroom, and shimmied into our colorful TT-brand tenniswear, we headed for the courts.

A lady drill instructor in aerobics gear led six of us in these awesome warmup exercises that combined yoga stretches with Diemeresque calisthenics. It was like Body by Jake meets Kundalini with Gurmukh. Way excellent, if you wanted to lose weight liquidly. I mean, you sweated off these Evian quarts. I gave Olga, the ponytailed Russian blond, like an 8.5 for energetic leadership. And a 9.8 for sadistic stamina. The woman's arms were the size of De.

Next we hobbled over to the court where our tennis ability was going to be tested and ranked by official USTA standards. The days, weeks, and months of blowing off P.E. had taken their toll. Public humiliation awaited us.

"Excuse me," Amber called out to Monica, the sleek, dark Betty with the clipboard who was slated to put us through our paces. "I can probably get my tennis instructor from Hillcrest to fax you my ranking. I'm like bitterly winded from Rasputin's workout and struggling for breath viciously irritates my deviated septum, which was supposed to be fixed two nose jobs ago."

"This won't be too bad," Monica promised. "Give it a try, okay?"

"Nazi," Amber hissed, stomping to the baseline.

Miraculously we all wound up at the advanced beginner end of the spectrum, a phrase which had at least one decent word in it. After tryouts we were segregated according to our rankings. Basically, Amber, De, and I *were* the advanced beginners. I looked for Tony while we waited for our court assignments and finally asked Monica if he was going to work with us.

"He'll definitely stop by at some point," she promised. "He's with the tournament level players right now. Over there." She pointed an Olympic-length juliette at one of the far courts, and there was my racquet-wielding babe blasting these serious power serves over the net. The ball moved so fast you couldn't even spot it. You just heard this explosive *thwack!* and saw a burst of green clay erupt where the yellow bomb had landed. "You'll be with Smoky Lawrence today. He's that cute guy on court three."

We gazed toward our reserved venue. A chronic Maxwell, with sunbleached dreads exploding from his white bandanna and pecs of steel straining his Lacoste, was wheeling a shopping cart full of practice balls onto the court.

De raised her Bada shades and studied the boy. "Awesome," she murmured. "If he's for beginners, imagine the Denzel advanced players get."

We shouldered our tennis racquets and headed toward court three. "Anyone need to freshen their SPF?" I inquired, offering safeguarding sunscreen to my teammates.

"Adios acrylics." De was in pre-mourning for the faux nails she'd recently had installed. But she borrowed my environment-friendly aerosol pump spray and shpritzed protectively.

"And *arrivederci* volumizer mousse," Amber added. "My hair's already wilted two sizes."

Dionne bonded with Smoky in a hot minute. You could practically hear the click of their mutual attraction. It was as loud as the sonic boom of Tony's serve. Before our hour was up, they were laughing together and scheming Murray's downfall. I was way impressed that my bud had chosen the candid road rather than pretending there was no boo in her background. Smoky could not have cared less. He thought De was more entertaining than spring break; thirty-two flavors and then some.

But the boy was not so distracted that he forgot to work us. We started lite with your basic racquet-back, eye-on-the-ball activity and progressed to the fatiguing leg and shoulder drudgery of lean-into-the-shot and follow-through. An eternity later was there an uncomplaining muscle left in our toned and slender bods? Not even.

"I am definitely doing the hot tub," Amber said as we limped off the clay, too tired even to holster our racquets.

My pink-and-gray graphite composite with kinetic mass was like draggin' in the dirt.

De dawdled with Smoky. I checked the far courts, but Tony had so moved on. A hot tub sounded chronic, but not until I'd showered off the day's green dust. Still, I mindlessly followed Amber's tangerine tennis dress toward the rec area.

"Duh, hello." She slammed on her Reebok brakes, pebbles flying from her biomechanically cushioned heels. "Welcome to second-rate world, where deprivation is an art," she grumbled, throwing her racquet into the dirt.

"Excuse me, to what do we owe this Prozac moment?" I inquired.

Too disturbed to speak, she did this exasperated, stiff-armed move, pointing toward the sign fastened to the side of the hot tub. Temporarily Out of Service, it said. Sorry for the Inconvenience. "I had my heart furiously set on this," Amber whimpered.

"There's a tub in the bunkhouse," I tried to console her.

"Like duh. It's a *bath* tub, Cher," she snarled. "If I wanted a bath, I guess that would be so totally where I would have sped five minutes ago. Only I want a *hot tub*. A warm, stimulating yet soothing, hydrotherapeutic aqua massage ministered by countless little underwater jets and streams."

"Well, duh. It's out of order," I grumbled, my patience, like my muscles, way overworked. I turned on my K•Swiss griptors and stalked away.

This funky little jar full of wildflowers, obviously hand-picked, and a note from Tony were waiting on the doorstep when I got to my room. De wasn't back yet, so I had to yell, "Yes!" and shriek and jump up and down like a random stooge all alone. I tossed my racquet onto my bunk and reread the classic missive. "I warned you," it said. "Hope you're not too wiped to take a walk. Give me a call when you get in. Tony." Way rejuvenated, I grabbed my cell phone, flipped it open, and stood there, fingers poised above the dialing device.

The good news was my tennis babe clearly cared. The bad news was, hello, he'd left no forwarding number. Cruising the freeway to ecstasy, I'd been squished before my exit. I flipped shut my Motorola and flopped down onto my bed.

Chapter 9

*I*t was like I'd dozed off to a Kenny G solo and awakened an hour later at a Spice Girls concert. Somewhere a phone was ringing. De crashed through the door, screaming, "Vengeance is mine!" And Amber, roasted medium rare and trailing streams of water, splashed out of the bathroom.

My heart was racing as if George Clooney and Noah Wyle had done a tag-team cardiac resuscitation on me for some random *ER* special. "Oh, are you sleeping?" De asked.

"Oh, are you ballistic?" I responded, all cranky from being blasted awake. "Yes, hello, I was way past dozing. Excuse me"—I turned to Amber—"why are you flooding our rug?"

"I'm much too mellow to dignify that," the lobster-hued girl asserted. "I did a twenty-minute brew in that def hot tub and I'm majorly serene. You type-A personalities don't know how to relax."

"I thought the hot tub was out of order," I said.

"That's what the sign said, only it was so bogus. I enlisted the aid of about five other disappointed tennis drones who were looking for a revitalizing soak, and we totally fixed it. Hello, by flipping the switch on!"

"I'm going to crush Murray," De confided gleefully. Fully pumped, she flung her tennis visor like a terry-cloth Frisbee onto our dresser. "Murray and Sean both! Smoky's promised to help me. Did you ever hear of Bobby Riggs? Smoky told me all about the man. He was just like Murray. This male chauvinist tennis player who claimed he could beat the best woman in the game. Who, back then, was Billy Jean King. And she so destroyed him."

"Did I hear a phone ringing?" I asked, still fuzzy and full of grit from the day's play. I hauled myself to my feet with a shower in mind.

"In addition to fine tuning my skills, Smoky's going to snag me a monster doubles partner," De ranted.

"Tony," Amber said.

"No," said De. "A female. There's this killer girl at camp who's won like every tournament she's ever played. Smoky says—"

"Hello—I mean he called," the wet one amended with exasperation.

"Who, Smoky?" De asked.

"Tony," Amber repeated, rolling her eyes. "He phoned for Cher. I told him you couldn't be disturbed," she informed me. "I mean, you were majorly zoned. I certainly wasn't going to wake you. And given that display of temper when you *were* awakened, how right was I to let sleeping dogs lie?"

I stopped in my tracks. Which happened to run right through the middle of one of Amber's puddles. A barrage of possible responses assaulted my brain, most of them ugly. Instead, I took a deep breath and went, "Did he like leave a number?"

"Said he'd catch you later," she said flippantly. "Oh, and you can't use the shower now. I've got to blow dry."

I didn't catch up with Tony until dinner. It was served family style in the rustic club house dining room. It was this total carbo load which, according to Zone experts, is such a no-no for the last meal of the day. I could hardly focus on the pasta parade, anyway. My cosmetically correct eyes were scanning the globe like CNN, desperately seeking Tony.

In the hopes of running into the hottie, I was garbed in slinky pink satin hip huggers with a white linen cut-lace blouse jacketing my pink bandeau. My long, freshly laundered locks were center parted into double ponytails, which draped langorously over my slender, slightly sore shoulders. Actually, there were few muscle groups not inflamed by the day's chores.

I was picking high-cal avocado cubes out of my salad when at last he walked in. Dipping my French nails in a glass of water and hastily napkining them dry, I waved to the buff boy. He was in baggy nylon running shorts and a Hawaiian print shirt, which hung open over his sunny bare chest. Sockless suede sneakers by Simple completed the wicked surfer boy ensemble.

Scuffing suedely through the dining hall, he nodded to the smiling faces that turned toward him like flowers to the sun. He grinned, nodded, slapped fives, snagged a piece of lettuce from someone's salad, grabbed a celery stick to munch. But he appeared oblivious to my hand signals.

Sheepishly I lowered my arm. Invisible is so not my best look.

"Tony at twelve o'clock," De murmured, poking me. "Did he see you?"

"Hello, she was like doing a total Statue of Liberty. How could he not have noticed?" Amber pointed out, pushing away her practically untouched salad. "Yet he is so not speeding in our direction." Like a lizard, the girl's color seemed to have faded from hot tub pink to pale pistachio. She did not look well. Which was so like, give me news not history.

De studied my former fan for a moment. "Tscha!" she said, snapping her fingers, "Could he be all dazed and confused because you never returned his call?"

"Girlfriend!" I stood up and buzzed De's adorably pigtailed head. "That is like the most genius deduction." My t.b. was a brutal brainer. The Agassi thought I'd blown him off. He was surfing a crushing rejection wave, getting sucked down into some bleak shame spiral. On a total EMS mission, I picked my way between the tables and headed for the baffled babe.

Tony was chatting with this green-hued boy with beads of sweat dotting his brow. "Must be something I ate," the boy croaked.

Monica of the rankings sat next to him. "But you hardly ate anything," she was saying.

"Maybe we should call someone," Tony suggested, then glanced up. Our eyes met. Then his sort of glazed over. But I couldn't help grinning at him.

"If you do," I said, "don't forget to leave your number so they can call you back."

He blinked. And then he smiled. Everything smiled. His whole face and hair and Hawaiian shirt and like his eyes went from that glazed stare to this gleaming greenish brown, all crisply sparkling and alive. Monica took one look at him and said, "Go on, Tony. I'll take care of Martin."

We left the dining room and walked along the pebbled path dividing the rows of nearly deserted tennis courts. Two players, Smoky and a girl who looked about ten years old, were hitting balls on a back court. The girl seemed way skilled for her size. Tony said she was one of the best players on the junior tour, and that her name was Bambi. Which was way appropriate since she moved around the court like an awkward young deer on legs that seemed miles too long for her body. Her arms, as her racquet connected with the ball, rippled sleekly, like hot fudge over rocks.

Other than the sound of their Penns and Wilsons bouncing in the background, the night was pretty still. It wasn't quite night. Pastel streaks of pink and gold still lit the sky. And it wasn't all still. Behind the courts, crickets and frogs were telling secrets in the woods. We walked side by side.

"I didn't leave my number?" Tony said as we followed the path around the courts and over toward the pool area.

"Nope. Not on the note and not with Amber when you phoned," I told him.

"Bummer."

"Way," I confirmed.

"It's that concussion you gave me at Neiman-Marcus. I haven't been able to think straight since." We moved across the pool's slate patio. I kicked off my excellent faux tortoise Jourdan sandals and dipped my toes into the water. It felt good to cool my feet. "So how'd your science cram session go?" Tony asked.

"Brutally aced my midterm," I told him. "I had to. Daddy wouldn't have let me come here otherwise."

"I guess that makes me a good influence on you."

"The bomb," I agreed, laughing. We watched the breeze rippling the water for a while, and I wound up filling Tony in on Daddy, who is your basic overprotective parent. Daddy screens all my prospective dates. I mean, *seriously* screens, as in checking credit ratings, bank statements, disciplinary records, administering Breathalyzer tests, and sometimes demanding a credit card deposit left in his care until I'm returned in excellent working order at curfew.

"Daddy can seem kind of harsh if you don't really know him, but he's a total pussycat. Plus he's a frantic tennis fan," I added, because the boy had grown way introspective. "And anyway, you *are* an excellent influence. I mean, I worked really hard to get here."

"I'm glad." Tony grabbed a towel off the poolside stack and handed it to me. "And now that you're here?" he asked as I blotted my pedicured toes. "How're you feeling? I mean, after the day's workout."

I slipped back into my Jourdans, and we followed the curve of the pebbled path back toward the clubhouse. "A little wiped, I guess. But everyone was totally dope. Monica and Smoky and even Olga the bonecrusher. It was a fun day."

It was almost dark now. But there were all these little lights lining the walk. Smoky and Bambi were still lobbing balls back and forth, and the woodland crew was still chirping, but the air was crispy and felt quiet.

"Too bad the hot tub's out of commission," Tony said. "The pool guy has to adjust the pH or something."

"Hello, my friend Amber apparently pulled a posse

together and renovated it this afternoon. She came back viciously parboiled."

We were about a yard from the building. Tony stopped and stepped in front of me. The golden boy tucked a lock of hair behind his ear. In the fading light the diamond stud's five-carat gleam was way hypnotic. "What would your father do if I kissed you?" he asked.

I tossed my head and brushed back one of my ponytails. "You don't even want to know," I said. We were standing like that, kind of swaying toward each other, when this shout went up from the dining hall deck.

"Cher!" It was Dionne's voice.

I started to respond, but Tony touched my mouth and went, "Wait," and the next thing I knew, his arms were around me. And his soft, friendly lips found mine.

"Where were you?" De demanded the minute I got back to our room. "I was looking for you. Amber's about to blow chunks. She's locked in the bathroom now, but she's been gasping and moaning like the English Patient. It's a total Academy Award performance. I think she ate something ripe. And you just basically bailed on me, left me alone with the death of fashion."

"I was with Tony," I confessed. "De, I'd never knowingly abandon you to deal with something this icky alone."

"You were with Tony all this time?" My t.b.'s stressed face brightened. "I totally forgive your desertion, but only if you tell me everything," she bargained. "Plus we're going to have to fax the Makeup Center. That stay-put lip gloss you were wearing at dinner is extremely gone. Now dish."

Amber charged out of the latrine when I was halfway though my choice narrative. "I think I've got the flu," she croaked. Her naturally pasty complexion had taken a turn for the worse. She looked like Marilyn Manson meets the Vampire Lestat. "Call Harrison for me. Tell him to come pick me up."

"What about your dad," De suggested. "I mean, he's a doctor. He'll know what to do."

"Hello, Earth to Dionne. He would totally quarantine me. And anyway, I bitterly miss my big cuddly."

A gag reflex is a terrible thing to waste. Nevertheless, De and I controlled ours. "It's late, Amber," I ventured. "Can you wait until morning?"

"Sure. Then Dr. Kevorkian can pick me up instead. Duh, hello, I'm dying."

We managed to get her into her bunk. Then, promising to be in regular cellular contact with my best bud, I went looking for Tony or Monica or someone who could help Amber. Who I met was the green kid from the dining hall. He was sitting on the steps of the bungalow next to ours, wrapped in a blanket and waiting, he said, for the nurse to come.

A nurse sounded like just the person we needed, too. So I speed dialed De, filled her in, and then perched a healthful distance from the boy and made candy-striper conversation. His name was Martin. When I mentioned that my roommate Amber was sick, too, he went, "Ugh. She's the dork who talked us into taking a hot tub today. Me and this guy Jason, who was also like spewing tonight. And these two women from Sweden who, I noticed, didn't even make it down to dinner."

"Sounds like an epidemic," I said mindlessly.

About a minute later Monica showed up. "Okay, Martin, Yvonne will be right here," she told him. "Can you hang on for another five? How're you doing?"

"You mean other than a killer stomachache, chills,

nausea, and sporadic hurling?" The poor boy shrugged his blanket-shawled shoulders. "Perfect, I guess."

Monica laughed and patted his head gently. I smiled appreciatively, but something he'd said sounded so déjà vu. Whatever it was disappeared as I reported to Monica that our roomie was also ailing. But when I described the hot tubby one's symptoms, the been-there, done-that feeling returned. Stomach cramps, bouts of spewing, chills, fevers, and a host of other fabulous flulike symptoms. Where had I heard that before?

Yvonne showed up just as I was dialing De to give her an update. Instead, I filled the nurse in on Amber's condition and whereabouts and rushed back to our room to join my bud.

Our poached roommate was moaning in her sleep, doing her Ralph Fiennes, unbandaged, imitation. De was Juliette Binocheing at bedside, sponging the dozing girl's sticky forehead.

"Girlfriend, I've got this yucky feeling. It's like when you know something but can't quite wrap your gray matter around it?" I told her.

"Hello, that was so me and science last semester," De said.

I blinked at her. "Science," I mused. "De, it has got something to do with science."

"Like pH factors and gram stains and hydrophilic organisms?"

I was nodding my head like mad. "But it's also about Amber and this kid Martin, who's got the flu—"

"Was it Professor Plum with a hammer in the study or Mrs. Peacock in the kitchen with a rope?" De teased me, citing one of our favorite childhood board games.

"That would be Clue," I retorted, "and I am hopelessly clueless." And then I shrieked, "It's salmonella!"

"What, like in the pantry with a gun?"

"No, De! In the hot tub with Amber and Martin and whoever else is curled up cramping tonight. De, I bet the reason the hot tub was off was that it needed to be cleaned. I mean," I said, remembering suddenly, "Tony said something about the pH being out of whack."

Could that be it? Had Amber and her pals sucked up some scummy water loaded with lethal microbes? The pieces were coming together. I was back in my den the night Harrison grilled us on how to differentiate microscopic organisms. Once again I heard Ambular listing the havoc salmonella could wreak. It was the same roll call of heinous symptoms she and green Martin were sharing tonight.

Suddenly it all made sense. "Salmonella loves water like Harry loves brisket," I said.

"It's way hydrophilic," De agreed, starting to get psyched now. But it was still just a hunch. To test my theory, we'd have to check the hot tub. And, silly us, we hadn't packed a microscope for tennis camp.

Still, every hot tub had a pH measuring apparatus. If everything was okay, the device would be balanced between left and right, alkaline and acid. If the gauge had swung to the left, it would mean the water in the tub was way alkaline, I reminded my bud as we hurriedly browsed our meager travel wardrobes for outerwear to guard against the night's chill. De slipped into this yummy yellow Christian Blanken cotton cardigan while I chose a skinny ribbed cashmere by Versus.

"So, if you're right," De said as, stylishly weatherized, we followed the pebbled path out toward the pool area, "and the pH gauge shows that the water is in the alkaline zone—"

"Then there's this major chance that those little red dots are in there oscillating," I told her, "splashing up a crippling microscopic storm."

"Science is so fun," De acknowledged as we checked the hot tub's pH apparatus. "Is it left or right?" she asked, peering over my shoulder.

"Right. It's like way alkaline," I confirmed.

"Tscha!" we exclaimed as one, and slapped these ferociously triumphant high fives.

It was after midnight by the time we divulged all—first to Yvonne and then to Monica, Tony, the EMS personnel who carted off Amber and her hot tub crew, the emergency room staffers at Cedars of Malibu Hospital and, finally, Dr. Salk, Ambu-lame's dad, who thanked us mega-profusely for salvaging his, fortunately, sole daughter.

As the last ambulance disappeared through the tennis camp archway, Tony took my hand and walked me back to my bungalow.

"Cher, you and De saved those kids tonight," the proper pro insisted. "And you saved me, too. My reputation, my career, this camp. Whew." He shook his classic head. "I don't even want to think about how bad it could've been. Even Yvonne thought we were dealing with some random but basically harmless flu."

I was furiously fatigued, yet wildly pumped by the night's events. "You did your part, too," I reminded him, pulling my pink Versus more tightly around my shoulders. "I mean, if you hadn't been all cute and concerned about our cranial collision, I wouldn't have been stoked about coming to your clinic. And without that incentive, acing science would so not have been a priority."

The grateful boy graced me with this golden look. "Scraping skulls with you was the best thing that's happened to me since I won the Australian Open. Which reminds me," he added, his voice losing its upbeat edge. "You know, I'm leaving for Australia on Monday."

"The day after the clinic ends?" The unexpected bulletin stirred an icky mood-swing in me. "No, I didn't know. That's in like three days. See, I'm good at math, too," I added, determined to upgrade our spirits with a joke. It wasn't exactly HBO's *Comic Relief,* but I was not about to let disappointment overwhelm this basically def moment.

"I wish we had more time together," Tony said, so reading my mind.

"Me, too," I admitted, squeezing his hand as we stepped into the beacon of light coming from my quarters.

De was on the porch, cellularly relating the details of our excellent science adventure to Murray. She gazed up at us and winked. Tony gave her a thumbs-up sign.

"Hang on, Murray," De said, covering the mouthpiece. "Are you sure it's okay?" she asked Tony.

"I owe you big," the tennis stud said.

"Okay, Murray." De got back on with her own private Bobby Riggs. "So, if you and Sean want to meet Tony Trilling and play a couple of sets with me and my partner, Tony says you can come up Sunday, which is our last day here. My partner?" She bit her lip to keep from breaking up. "Oh, she's just this little, bitty girl named Bambi. Go back to sleep. I'm sorry I woke you. I'll beep you tomorrow," De finished up, yawning now.

Tony and I were leaning against the porch railing.

"Helping out Dionne was easy," he said to me. "But how am I going to thank you for being such an awesome microbe hunter? You guys saved lives tonight and did everyone at camp a monster solid."

"Cher's a natural born do-gooder," De said, opening the screen door and yawning again. "If I'm going to work with Smoky and Bambi tomorrow . . . Make that today," she said, glancing at her sports Swatch, "I'd better bail and catch some zees. As Bono would say, U2, girlfriend? Another day of arduous fun and painful play awaits us."

My weary big was right.

"Better go," Tony regretfully agreed. "If you're going to be as slammin' a ball player as you are a scientist, you've got to get some rest," the babe said, giving me that classic billboard grin.

"I am so Audi," I acquiesced. "Catch you later." I started for the door, but the tennis hunk held on to my hand.

"You didn't answer my question," he softly reminded me. "How am I going to repay you? Think about it, okay, Cher?"

"Oh, I'll come up with something," I teased him.

He squeezed my hand gently, then smoothed back my hair, which I was sure the night air had furiously volumized. Then leaning forward, he brushed his choice, warm lips across my brow. "Anything," he promised.

Chapter 10

*H*ow awesome has my serve become?" De asked. After a day of grueling athletic improvement, my t.b. and I were poolside, legs dangling in the sun-splashed, chlorinated water. We were refilling our depleted moisture content with rejuvenating iced teas.

"It's like brutally Steffi," I affirmed, between sips of the cool herbal brew. "And my forehand slice?" I asked.

"Way Gabriela," De exulted, setting down her tall glass to spray another glossy coat of sunscreen onto her Armaya Arzuaga bikini–clad bod. "Coach Diemer would be so moved. She'd totally plotz."

The mention of our stained science sub triggered a twinge of remorse in me. I peered at my homey through the dark lenses of my choice cK shades, feeling momentarily unworthy of the classic new OMO Norma Kamali stretch plaid swimwear draping my flawless frame. "We owe her," I reminded my bud. "I mean, the violet streak in her hair can be viewed as an improvement, but basically, De, we did trash the woman, purpley disfiguring her face."

"And demolishing her one semidecent suit," De acknowledged, "even if it was just a generic faux Armani."

The random feeling passed quickly. I am so not good at guilt. Wallowing is my least favorite sport. I fully believe in focusing on the solution, not the problem. So that's what I decided to do.

We were perched at pool's edge, sluggishly exercising our submerged and aching limbs. The afternoon's tennis activities hadn't left much time for musing. But now, therapeutically kicking out the day's kinks, an answer to Tony's query began to take form in my mind. And it had Ms. Diemer's name all over it.

"De, what would make coach Diemer frantically happy? What does she really need?" I asked, growing excited as my vision took shape.

"Would a makeover, liposuction, and a personal shopper be what you had in mind?" my bud replied.

"Not even."

"It was just a guess," De said defensively.

"You know that underfunded tennis crew she coaches? How buff would it be if America's most outstanding practitioner of the game personally shared his strategies and secrets with them?"

De's feet stopped flapping in the water. "Hello? Are you saying what I think you're saying? You mean, if Tony coached Ms. Diemer's destitute dream team?"

"It's a thought," I said.

"That's not a thought," my primary big said, grinning supportively, "that is the bomb, a brainstorm, the totally deepest idea du jour."

"Then you're in favor?" I laughed.

"How many votes do I get?" De asked, throwing her sleek, SPF-slathered arms around me and administering a monster congratulatory hug. "But where and when? Tony's off to Australia right after camp, isn't he?"

"Yes. But what if we could get Diemer's gang up here on Sunday, the last day of the clinic?"

"Hello. You mean the day young Bambi and I are scheduled to to give my boastful boo and his comical sidekick a tragic tennis lesson? Cher, that would be so trippin'. Imagine having an entire herd of spectators viewing that decisive match? A fan faction led by our frantically pro-femme P.E. coach?"

"That's harsh, De," I evaluated my bud's plan. "But doable. I like it. More important, I think the idea will appeal to Ms. Diemer. After all, she's the one to whom we owe amends."

"Let's call her right after our swim," De said. So we clinked our iced tea glasses, took a final, refreshing gulp, and threw caution to the wind. Synched and psyched we dived headfirst into the hair-punishing pool.

By the time we got back to our room, dechlorinated, shampooed, conditioned, styled, moisturized, and applied even the most minimal makeup, just like eye stuff mainly, with the merest shimmer of protective powder blush, it was too late to catch the coach at school. So we tried the number she'd left on her voice mail.

Doing something decent for Ms. Diemer was, as the saying goes, simple but not easy. The jockette was in an uproar when she returned our beep. "This is an emergency-only number," she hollered above the whoosh and squeal of traffic noises.

"Where are you, Ms. Diemer, on a freeway?"

Wrong question. It further inflamed the irate coach. "Not everyone has a car phone, Horowitz."

"Duh, I know that, Ms. D. Car phones are like way obsolete. Viciously yesterday. Like beepers."

"I'm not *on* the freeway." She brutally cut me off. "No. I had to pull *off* the freeway. I had to find a *pay* phone. I had to drop half my salary into said phone. Of course, I *was* on the freeway." The P.E. czar was half hissing, half hollering. "I *was* driving out to my after-school program to work with the few, the proud, the *deserving* kids who actually value my experience and expertise."

De's skull was smushed up against mine. The two of us were trying to share a single, slim Motorola. "That's exactly what we wanted to talk to you about, Ms. D.," Dionne suddenly interjected.

"Who is that?" Diemer demanded.

"That was De," I informed her as my manic bud practically yanked the phone out of my hand.

"Hola, Ms. D. We've got the most excellent idea," De announced. And then this archaic series of rings and dings and like surfing echoes hit the line.

"Yeeww, what's that?" De asked, pushing the phone back against my ear.

The noise was fully annoying. "Hello, that's the operator cutting into Ms. D's call," I explained. "She's demanding an additional coinage drop."

"Really?" De was bewildered. She hadn't used a pay phone, well, maybe ever. I had, once, when I'd gotten stranded at a party in the Valley. Don't even ask what I was doing in the Valley. It is way too painful. Suffice it to say, I was so not seeking Mr. Right.

124

"Doesn't she even have a phone card?" De asked, aghast. "What do they pay these people?"

"Ms. Diemer, Ms. Diemer, don't hang up," I urged. "Is there a number on that phone? We'll call you back. Or you can call us collect!"

"What's she doing?" De wanted to know.

"I think she's putting money in the machine. Coins. You know, like you use for the metered parking on Rodeo."

"Like who uses?" De was indignant. "Cher, I park valet and get my receipts stamped."

Finally the coin assault ended and Ms. Diemer was back on the line. "Okay, you've got one minute to explain yourselves," she grumbled.

So we did. And Ms. D. got all quiet. And we had to go, like, "Hello, anyone home?" So then we heard this humongous honk. And De went "Yeeww! What was that?" And I didn't say anything, but I knew it was Ms. Diemer blowing her nose and that the brawny babe was furiously choked with tears and gratitude.

"I'll get back to you," she barked brusquely. And it was over.

De and I received a standing ovation at dinner that night. I was so glad I'd chosen this slithery lace confection that Shalom Harlow had modeled on the cover of *W.* And my hair was all lustrous and loose, with the def swing and bounce of a Salon Selectives ad. There was so little time left to leave a lasting impression on my tennis hottie. Every moment and outfit counted. And my little lace Versace was fully indelible. De turned heads, as well, in her huggably adorable sleeveless Chanel. We strolled into the clubhouse fashionably late, somewhere between soup and salad, and were totally amazed by the applause.

Tony was the first to hit his Reefs-sandaled feet. And then like Olga the ham-armed exersseuse stood, and Monica of the decorative two-inch acrylics, and by the time Smoky was up, everyone in the hall was clapping and whistling for us. It was so sweet and familiar. Just like school. Like those countless days we'd arrive sporting some choice new ensemble or classically styled 'do and everyone would break out in spontaneous acclaim.

But here, away from home and a solid fan base, De and I were totally stooged by the fuss. I was all, "Thank you, thank you, this is so mad of you guys."

"All we did was like save a couple of measly lives," De modestly protested.

All of a sudden flashbulbs started to pop. And who should appear when the dancing amoebas cleared from our vision but Abigail, Tony's pro-Armani PR flack, the very Betty who'd lured us to camp in the first place. In homage to our rustic surroundings, the babe was in casualwear, a vintage black cotton crocheted halter top mini that looked way Gucci, and of course, she was toting her signature clipboard.

"Are you postal?" Blinking gingerly, De scolded the black-clad photographer who stood beside Abby. "You almost blinded us, to say nothing of demolishing our eye makeup."

"Hey," the guy said, hoisting his Nikon for another blast, "I do what I'm told. I'm just following instructions."

"My instructions," Abigail confessed. "I thought it'd be a brilliant PR coup to do a story on your heroism here in Tonyville."

De and I glanced at each other. "Hello, I don't think so," I said.

126

"Don't be humble," Abby urged, with the same, dark-lipped smile that had lifted the credit cards right out of our red Vuitton Epi leather wallets and won our signatures on tennis clinic contracts that fateful Neiman's afternoon.

But we were older and wiser now. "Not even," De said. "Humble, schmumble. All I need is for my mom to find out we were toying with lethal bacteria, doing a sleep-away in Salmonella State Park. I don't think so."

"It's a lawsuit waiting to happen," I concurred, "and Daddy would take it on in a hot minute, plus totally squash any future plans I might have to like ever be out of his sight."

Abby was about to wheedle. I could see her cranking for ways to alter our decision. Fortunately, Tony rushed to our aid. "Abs, I don't think we want to advertise this situation," he broke it to her gently. "Think it through, man. Welcome to Tony Trilling's Toxic Tennis Camp?"

"You're young but you're right. I was just trying to put spin on a dire situation. Okay, Carlos." She called off her camera-wielding Doberman. "Let's eat."

The paparazzo Abigail had leashed did manage to grab some action shots of me. It was after dinner. Tony and I had gone for our semitraditional post-chow stroll. With his granite arm slung around my sleeveless shoulder, we were bonding out where the air was clear and the interruptions few.

Tony was all squeaky clean and closely shaved. A fragrant tang of his cologne mingled with the woodsy scent of our surroundings. There was also the lightest bite of chlorine wafting from the pool, which was underwaterly lit and sending up these romantic, rippling reflections. So, when I glanced at Tony's bristle-free face as we stood side by side on the slate patio, kind of staring idly into the water, he looked younger than usual and the teensiest bit eerie and green.

I had hoped to avoid the what-happens-after-Sunday chat I sensed was coming.

"I'm really going to miss you, Cher," Tony started it. "I travel around so much. I hardly ever get to know anyone—"

Hello, a hundred 'zine and newspaper photos of Tony huddling with world-class babes leaped to mind. And the tournament videos of wide-eyed blonds and slinky brunettes watching from the stands, hiding their eyes or gnawing off their French nails if bandanna boy blew a shot. And, of course, that memorable MTV birthday special, narrated by Jenny McCarthy, where the guest list was wall-to-wall known Bettys.

Tony must have caught my skeptical look.

"I mean, *really* get to know someone," he amended, turning to give me one of his hyper-sincere, hypnotic, hazel-eyed gazes. He took my shoulders in his callused hands. "Someone like you. Someone in my general age range, who's like still in high school. I went to three different schools in one year when I started playing tournaments. I never even graduated. My dad tutored me on tour for a while. Then I had a full-time tutor. I got a degree last summer but no cap and gown, no sitting on stage with a bunch of friends."

My clear blue eyes were totally locked on that famous yet increasingly fresh face. And I could feel his grip heating my deltoids. "I guess you missed a lot," I commiserated, trying not to stare at those full, slightly parted lips. "My t.b.'s are the total best. But then, none of them has ever like won major trophies and gotten kissed on both cheeks by international royalty and had their every shot beamed if not heard round the world."

"Cher, I wish we could—" Tony began. Then the boy's face brutally blurred as he swooped down to kiss me. And that was when Carlos, the paparazzo, snapped this jarring series of pics. His shutter clicked and whirred, the flashbulb going off again and again. The first blinding burst of light startled us. Tony and I struck teeth, scraped lips, and uttered little bruised yelps, yet we were way reluctant to break out of this stunningly memorable kiss. Finally we came up for air. Gingerly touching his battered lips, Tony yelled to Carlos, "Hey, stop that, man."

The photographer disappeared into the woods behind the pool. Tony started after him, then stopped and turned back to me. "Are you okay? What's that noise?" he asked.

"Whoops. My cellular." I realized, coming to. I fumbled for the slimline tucked in my Fendi woven leather drawstring purse. "Hello," I said. I guess my voice was kind of woozy. My bruised lips were still tingling.

"Horowitz?" Ms. Diemer's voice was loud but unsure. "Is that you?"

"Hi, Ms. D.," I said. "So, did you talk to your crew?"

"We'll be there. Every single one of them. And me, of course. If I have to rent a bus, we'll be there."

"Hold on a sec, Tony," I said, this smile stealing across my puffy lips at just the sight of him. "Do you think we could throw in transportation?"

"Is that your gym teacher?" he asked, brushing my bangs back and planting this feathery soft kiss on my forehead. "Let me speak to her," he said.

I passed him the phone. "Hey, is that Ms. Diemer?" he said. "This is Tony Trilling. Cher's told me so much about you and all the good work you're doing with that after-

129

school program. So am I going to get to meet you and those kids on Sunday? We can send out a van to pick you all up.''

They chatted for a couple of seconds more. And as I told De later that night, I knew that long after the purple had faded from Ms. Diemer's cheeks, that call would be remembered. Tscha! We had totally made her day.

Chapter 11

*P*urple or not, you could hardly see Ms. Diemer's face anyway. When the vans pulled into tennis camp
on Sunday, the coach was wearing this Bronson Alcott
baseball cap pulled down low on her tie-dyed head. But
under the brim of that cap, you could so tell she was
smiling. The eight- and nine-year-olds who tumbled out of
the vans were, too. Each outfitted with a tennis racquet,
they came in all colors, shapes, and sizes, like leggings at
Express, fully fitting in with the camp's international flavor.

"This is the stuff I want you to photograph," Abigail told
Carlos, who'd returned from his midnight hike. "The Tonys
of Tomorrow. It's got zing. Spin. Panache, no?"

"Whatever," Amber remarked, rolling her bovine brown
eyes. The recuperating girl had arrived moments earlier.
Harrison, looking way Orange County in madras Bermudas
and a pink Lacoste shirt, was wheeling the disgruntled
invalid's chair. It was a temporary throne. For her first

public outing, the clueless one had chosen a boldly striped canvas ensemble that looked as if it had been cut from a fruit store awning. Between that and the way she was snapping at Harry and ordering him around, you could tell that Amber was so on the mend, practically her egregious old self again.

"Hey, Harry." De slapped hands with the plastic surgery heir. "Are you here to watch the Match of the Century, me and my diminutive partner?" She pointed out Bambi, who except for those lengthy legs, looked like you could fold her up and take her home in a backpack. Lethargically volleying at the net with Smoky, the slender girl was clearly conserving her energy for the main event. "We'll be teaming up to take on Duh and Duh-er." De indicated Murray and Sean, who were warming up on Court Four.

The contenders had arrived *en crew,* with Jesse, Ringo, Jared, Ben, Brian, and Morrissey in tow. The boys were now arrayed on the Court Four bleachers, all except for Ringo, who was strolling the pebbled path toward the pool with Janet. The fully rebonded pair were holding hands. Their entwined fingers reminded me of my own digitally clenched walks with Tony.

"Haw, haw, haw," Amber's soul mate guffawed in response to De's remarks. "You really expect to beat those big, strapping boys over there? As my honey always says, 'Hello, meathead, I don't think so.'"

"Meathead?" I whispered to De as the couple moved off toward the hot tub area, where Amber intended to milk further concessions from her benevolent bozo by giving him a tour of her tragedy. "Is that really what Amber calls him?"

"Excuse me, but how apt is it?" De responded.

I saw her point.

"Don't kiss me. Don't hug me. Don't even say hello. It's all right. Act like you don't know I'm alive."

We whirled around to face the voice that launched a thousand guilt trips. "Hi, Grandma. Good to see you," I said, prepared for a vicious pinch but leaning in anyway to buzz her surgically elevated face. Life with Elroy had mellowed her. I got close, planted one, and backed off without incident.

The condo czarina was flanked by Ringo's grandfather and my very own daddy. Bringing up the rear, carrying Grandma's alligator purse and auxiliary lightweight jacket, was everyone's favorite Boy Scout, Josh.

"Josh!" Dionne leaped at the boy, who did look kind of fresh. Josh is slim and rangy, and his rugged jawline thaws into dimples when he smiles, which is way too often. If the boy hadn't wasted his youth telling me there was life after shopping, I might have been more forgiving of his lame flannel look.

While De gave my faux bro a hearty welcome, I gave Daddy a huge hug. "What's wrong with your face?" Daddy demanded. "Your lips look all puffy."

"Allergies?" I suggested.

"Since when?"

"It's that lip gloss," De came to my aid. "We're never shopping MAC again. Or was it Nordstrom's? Hey, Mr. Horowitz, glad you could make it."

"Who is that?" Daddy whispered to me. He's always kidding around.

"Hello, it's Dionne, Daddy. My best friend since grade school," I played along. But to be fair, De had done a radical shift in hairstyle. In like this homage to Smoky, she and Bambi had decided to do dreads. It was a furiously Fugees look, part *Vogue*, part *VIBE*.

133

Daddy nodded. "I knew she looked familiar. Too bad about the other one, with the bad nose job."

"Amber," I said.

"She got sick, caught a bug or something?"

"Mr. Horowitz?" Everyone turned at once. Daddy, Grandma, Farbstein the elder. Josh, Dionne, Ms. Diemer and her crew, and me. Especially me.

Looking like a total shoe ad in his flaming bandanna and brightly colored tennis togs, his clean hair and monster earring catching sparks, sunlight picking up the blond stubble on his tanned cheeks, and those hazel eyes big and laughing—it was Tony. Everyone kind of gasped at the sight of him. The suck of air was so intense you could almost see his bandanna flutter. Only the teensiest flaw distorted his perfect features. This almost invisible nick on his lip attained during last night's kissing fiesta.

He stuck out his hand to Daddy. "I'm Tony Trilling," he said. "Glad you could make it, sir."

Daddy's everyday frown lifted right off and this chronic smile replaced it. "You're quite a kid, one of the good guys," he said, shaking Tony's hand. "Or so my daughter tells me."

Tony gave me this meltingly fine grin.

Daddy squinted at him suddenly. "What's wrong with your lip?" he asked suspiciously.

"Er, I scratched it . . . shaving," Tony said, fingering the love bruise.

"He shaves his lips?" Grandma demanded.

I took Tony's arm. "Sorry, Daddy, but we promised to help Coach Diemer's gang improve their game. Why don't you and Grandma and Josh and everyone go over to Court Four and watch De embarrass her high school honey?"

Tony and I herded Diemer's kids over to the front courts,

where he, Monica, and a crew of other staffers set them up for the clinic. I hung with them for an hour or so, wheeling carts of tennis balls onto the court, filling water cups, putting Band-Aids on scraped knees, and generally performing random hostess duties. Which only my resolve to aid Ms. Diemer made even thinkable. Servile is so not me. It's not like I'm *above it* or anything. I'm just menially limited. Anyway, after a while, the cheering and shouts from Court Four got increasingly persuasive. I didn't want to miss De's entire match.

"Go on," Tony said when I asked if he still needed me. "We're finishing up here anyway. I'll meet you at the game in five."

By the time I got there, Murray and Sean were breathing hard and showing definite signs of wear. Sean was spending way too much time hitching up his cut-off Rockets. In contrast to his partner's huge baggies, oversize nylon Lakers shirt, and Kani cap hooked backward on his head, Murray was in classic tennis whites. He looked way authentic, like a real pro, pouting and going postal just like McEnroe or Connors.

"Lookit the glare coming off of De's Armanis," he complained, tossing his racquet onto the court. "How can I play when the girl's eyewear is blinding me?"

"Yo, yo, yo." Sean stalked the backcourt, hiking up his billowing shorts and narrowing his eyes at the crowd. "Who's rattling that paper? How we supposed to focus if everyone's all making noise?"

Their playing partnership was as synched as their dress code. Bambi's rocketing strokes had them banging into each other. And the spin Smoky had added to De's kinder, gentler shots seemed to psych them to a standstill.

I watched from the sidelines for a while, then strolled

135

over to the bleachers and scooched in between Smoky, whose Ray•Bans were locked on the game, and Jesse, who was browsing through his portable CD collection. "What's the score?" I asked.

"Annoying," Jesse replied.

"If Bambi and Dionne take this one, they'll be ahead five games to three," Smoky informed me. "Then they need just one more to end it. But I don't like the way Bambi looks. She's got a weak ankle. She's getting wobbly."

I saw Tony, surrounded by Ms. Diemer's gang, heading toward us. I waved to him, then checked the court again, looking for the weakness Smoky had described. All I saw was Bambi smashing a serious one down the middle and watching it whistle past Murray and Sean.

"That is so not fair," Sean grumbled, pointing at the kids scrambling up into the bleachers. "All these mini peops running around, messin' with my concentration."

Janet leaned across Jesse, nearly capsizing his CD holder. "One more game and we win!" she shouted to me.

"Do you know how many golden oldies you almost dumped?" Jesse demanded. Hugging his CD stash protectively, he glared at her. "I've got a Smashing Pumpkins here from 1995."

"Cher, I want you to go in for the next game," Smoky said.

"Excuse me?" I remarked. Flattering as the proposal was, I had to be realistic. I had no desire to soil my classic sportswear or scuff my technologically superior shoes on the altar of stoogedom. Public humiliation is so not my calling. My cross court rallying and net volleys had improved in Tony's custody, and my serve, while breakable, was often accurate. But to ply those meager skills in full view of a postally pumped crowd was a total Not Even.

"Bambi's got an important tournament coming up. I don't want her damaging that ankle. I'm going to pull her," Smoky concluded.

"Hello, have you seen me play?" I queried.

"I have." Suddenly Tony was beside us. "You can do it, Cher. I don't know anything you *can't* do."

I gave my hottie a choice smile, but chose not to mention my recent science lab fiasco. I mean, how vital a life skill is flask-uncorking?

A huge cheer went up, signaling the end of the game. De and Bambi had taken another one. Now, as the slender girl grabbed a towel and left the court, I noticed that she was moving cautiously. It wasn't quite a limp, but she did seem to be favoring her left leg as she headed toward our end of the court. "Smoky," Bambi said, pressing her face against the wire fence, "my foot's bothering me."

"I caught it," he said, and turned to Tony.

"Girlfriend, did you see what Smoky's done to my serve?" De joined us. There was a towel slung around her neck, and a bottle of Evian in her grasp. She was furiously aglow, pumped with a fierce endorphin rush. "What's up?" she asked, glancing from me to Smoky.

Tony answered her. "We're going to pull Bambi. She can't play on that foot. It's not worth it. You guys played some awesome doubles, De, but Bambi's career is at risk."

"You mean we're going to quit now?" De's face fell. She glanced at Bambi, and I could see her struggling to pull herself together, to recapture her faltering grin. Guilt is so not De's game. She didn't want the spunky young girl to feel bad.

"I'm sorry, De," Bambi said softly. "I wish I could finish—"

Their wilted opponents were crashed out on folding

chairs a few feet from the net. Sean's head was flopped back, his face covered with a wet towel. His hairy legs were trembling in their chronic Wilson Pro Staff Extremes. Murray, tennis whites Sampras-ly soaked with sweat, was leaning forward, hands clenched between his knees.

Guys were calling to them from the stands. "Hey, what happened, man?" 'Wake up, Murray. They're killing us." 'You almost had them," a fan yelled encouragingly. But he was drowned out by a generic voice roaring, "You guys blow!"

The boy buds seemed so beaten I almost felt sorry for them. Until Murray looked up and saw us staring at him.

"Yo, whassup?" he hollered. "You girls folding on us? Can't take the pressure?" he challenged.

A volley of boos and catcalls greeted his heroics. Amber jumped out of her wheelchair on the sidelines and did this flamboyant thumbs-down. "Get over yourself, loser," she howled. The crowd was getting ugly. With the amoebically impaired one leading it, big surprise.

The fires of impending triumph that had brightened De's hazel orbs were dull now. She winced as she watched her man being dissed. She'd wanted the boy annihilated athletically, not verbally. "Bambi hurt her foot," she reported, with severely mixed emotions. "She can't finish the set."

"Yo, yeah, right!" Sean tore the towel off his face and leaped to his feet. "They folded. They crumpled. We killed them!"

"Not even!" De blazed, torn between pity and outrage.

"You wussin'?" Murray challenged her. "You tellin' me, you've had . . ."—he paused dramatically, cupped his hand to his ear and cocked his head at her—". . . enough?"

"Wussin'!" Sean cried. Relief had dealt him a sudden

energy surge. "Women always be wussin'. Shoppin' and wussin', that's what they're good at." He was over the top now. He balled up his towel, slammed it down, then raised his arms and did this gloating victory dance.

Murray joined him, stomping his feet and chanting, "They quit! They quit!"

"Hello!" I stood abruptly. "Who said anything about quitting?"

De spun toward me.

"Cher," Bambi whispered, wide-eyed.

Tony planted an iron grip on my waist and hoisted me out of the bleachers. "I knew you'd come through," he said, spinning me jubilantly for a moment, then administering a rib-crunching hug.

"Get out," De said. "You mean, you and me?"

"T h 's in fair weather and foul," I answered, slapping her a limp high five. "Anyway, you and Bambi have brutally worn the boys down. There's hardly anything left for me to do."

Tennis is a spectator sport. Like it's so fun when you're watching it on a digitally superior seventy-five inch monitor. But it is another game entirely when you're a player, running all over the court scuffing your ergonomically correct Keds while perspiration rinses the last vestige of volumizer from your hair and clay dust sandblasts the Cover Girl finish right off your face.

But I was not thinking of that as De and I trotted onto the court to the ballistically hyped cheers of our manifold fans. And there were many baritones among them, not even counting Coach Diemer.

It was Murray's turn to serve. I knew he put a lot of power behind his first shot, so I backed up, hunched forward, and swung my centrally held racket from side to side. It was an excellent pro parody. Crouched and waiting, I knew I'd gotten the stance right from the approving murmurs of the crowd.

Murray hefted the ball into the air, then swung down viciously on it. Keep your eye on the ball is like the first law of tennis. And I brutally obeyed it as the fuzzy sphere whirled toward me. Racquet back, I could practically hear Smoky say. Get that arm ready, a memory of Tony's voice urged me. And I did, then stepped into the shot, and to my total shock, the hurtling yellow orb found the center of my racquet and I whacked it back over the net, right past Sean. You could hear this *whiff* as the ball fired past the boy.

"That was so Steffi!" De greeted me, her racquet triumphantly raised. Then it was her turn to receive Murray's serve. The magic Smoky had wrought upon the girl was still working. With a Hingis-like accent on accuracy and control, Dionne returned the ball short, forcing her winded boo to rush netward. Unfortunately, Sean had the same idea. The homeys met head-on, tangling ankles in no-man's-land, their racquets crashing together as De's ball dribbled neatly over the net.

"Martina!" I saluted my bud. And a tradition was born. Each time we won a point, we called out the name of a celebrated female tennis hottie and victoriously slapped racquets to the whistles and cheers of our fans.

As the game progressed, however, I forced myself to tune out the congratulatory shouts of the bleacher Bettys. True tennis is so not an ego quest. It's a contest of fierce skill and judgment. And I needed all my concentration for decision-making, like was I going to totally trash my 'do loping full forward to catch a shot on the fly or protect against limp follicles by letting the ball bounce before I blasted it back?

Before I knew it, De was hollering, "This one's for Billy Jean!" and with a ferocious ground-stroke she totally Bobby Riggsed the boys, finishing them off neatly.

We'd won!

Pandemonium erupted in the stands. Chants of "Girls rule!" rocked the premises. De and I hugged each other and jumped up and down. Then we graciously jogged to the net to shake hands with our weary opponents.

"Excellent game," I said, extending my hand to Sean.

"A decisive victory for girlkind," De added.

"Yeah, it was okay," the boy grumbled. "I mean, we was toyin' with you for the first couple of games—"

"Excuse me?" De's eyebrows arched dangerously. She turned to Murray. "Is that what you think? You were toyin' with us?"

"I didn't say that." Murray's hands flew up in the defensive palms-out posture. "We played you, that's all," he said, a faint smile curling his fuzz-crowned mouth.

"Excuse me. One minute please." It was De. One stylishly julietted finger began to wave in front of Murray's face. Her other hand had assumed the hip position. And her dreadlocked head started to waggle. My homey was in serious debate stance. "What do you mean, you *played* us?" she demanded. "You mean like played us in tennis, or played us for fools? Because, if it's the latter, Murr-onic, let me straighten you out now."

Spectators began to pour onto the court, seeking autographs and celeb proximity. Many of them gathered ritually around Murray and De as the happy couple launched into one of their finest performances. A crowd quickly formed around them. Amber, back in her wheelchair, ordered Harrison to push her through the throng. "Bacterially disabled hot tub buff coming through," she called. "Let's suck in those abs and tighten those thighs, this chair's not stopping till it's valet parked, front row center."

Tony appeared. Rescuing me from a mob of Diemer's reverent midgets, he buzzed my flushed cheek. "You were awesome," he said. "Totally impressive." He said it softly because Sean was nearby, looking glum.

Brushing court clay from his dusty Rockets, Sean turned to Janet and Ringo for solace. "We weren't that bad," he said. "Word up, I mean, I uncoiled some nasty speed and power."

For a pair of severe IQs, Janet and Ringo so didn't comprehend the boy's need. "That game was so fun," Janet said. "You were totally hilarious, Sean."

Tony steered me around the trio. "I had the tennis camp diplomas made up for your teacher's team," he told me. "She's rounding up her gang and we'll make the presentations in the clubhouse. Will you help me with the ceremony?"

"Definitely," I said. I had thought it would be a choice touch to award each and every kid in Ms. Diemer's after-school program a certificate of graduation signed by Tony. Everyone was stoked at the notion. Ms. Diemer was thrilled. Abigail and Carlos would get a decent story out of the project. Tony said it would end the day and this camp session on an awesome up note. As we left the tennis court area, I only hoped that De, who knew my ulterior motive for pushing the plan, ended her debate with Murray in time to do her part.

I excused myself and ducked into my cabin for a quick

shower and emergency repairs on my hair and makeup. By the time I got down to the clubhouse, the tables had been cleared and a small stage set up at the far end of the dining hall. A flock of visitors had been pressed into service. Even Daddy was there, in a strictly supervisory position. He was showing Grandma, Elroy, and Josh where to set up the chairs, and hollering at Carlos to unload the certificate boxes next to the podium. Daddy is such a natural-born leader. It's one of the endearing qualities we furiously share. "Come on, Ray," he cheered Grandma on as she struggled to shlep a pair of wooden folding chairs up onto the platform. "It's good for you. It'll firm up those arms."

De showed up about a minute after Ms. Diemer and her rampaging herd of rug rats hit the hall. The kids fanned out in all directions until Ms. D. blew a blast on her whistle and collared one of their ringleaders. "Okay, Montoya," she ordered this squirming seven-year-old. "Hit the deck and give me twenty." Everyone quieted down then. Except for Montoya, who was showing off doing one-armed pushups for the coach. "See that?" she snarled at De and me. "And he's only seven years old."

"And way closer to the ground than us," De countered. "Anyway, that's what I really want, overdeveloped triceps." De turned to me. "Do you have the cap and gown?" she asked.

I nodded. "I'm going to spring it in a second, but first, let's get the kids up there." We herded Diemer's after-school crew up onto the platform and into their seats. The room began to fill with tennis camp personnel and students, and our visiting homeys. I hurried up to the podium. "We're ready to begin," I announced. "Where's Tony?"

My babe hopped onto the stage. "Before we start, De

143

and I have a present for you." De opened the box I'd stashed in the kitchen and pulled out a graduation cap and gown.

Tony laughed. "You guys must be kidding. You want me to wear that?"

"Totally," said De, helping him into the gown.

"You're going to be giving out diplomas, aren't you?" I took off the babe's bandanna and replaced it with a black mortarboard, the squared-off hat worn for formal graduation ceremonies. Viewed at a distance, my tennis man looked fully scholastic, like a total Phi Beta Kappa Keanu. I adjusted the gold tassel hanging from the brim of his board, then De and I took our seats, and Ms. Diemer got up and started reading off the names of the kids.

It was so cute. They were all serious and excited when Tony handed them their rolled-up, ribbon-tied certificates. Each one of them got a monster round of applause. And finally as Montoya, the micro-Schwarzenegger, received the last of the little diplomas, De and I leaped up to the podium.

"Tony, we've got a certificate for you, too," De announced, elbowing Ms. Diemer.

"Yes," the brawny coach sputtered, staring at this index card I'd written out for her. "It's for, er, graduating from being an . . . um."

"Totally props pro," I coached her.

"To becoming the, er . . ."

"Humanitarian hottie of the hour!" De shouted.

"You, Tony Trilling," I took over, "are the recipient of the first annual Cher Horowitz Do-Good diploma. Congratulations, Tony, you've earned it," I said, depositing the rolled-up paper into his callused palm.

All the kids on stage jumped up and started applauding

and cheering. Daddy urged them on. "Let's hear it. Put those hands together. That's my little girl. The Cher Horowitz Do-Good Award. I like it," he said. "We can call it a charitable trust and write off the camp fees."

Tony stood there basking in applause. "You remembered," he whispered to me. "You remembered that I never graduated."

"And never got to wear a cap and gown, and sit onstage with a bunch of friends," I said. "You told me that out at the pool. I remember everything about that night."

Just then flashbulbs started popping. "And I remember Carlos." Tony laughed. "I wonder what happened to the photos he took?"

I laughed, too. Then Tony put his arm around me, and he and De and I waved to everyone. Murray was standing in the front row, applauding like wild. De waved him up onto the stage, and he took her hand and raised it high over his head, as if to say, "You're the winner, De. You're the prize." And then, with flashbulbs blazing, in front of twenty-five kids, twelve classmates, the camp staff, Ms. Diemer, my grandma, and Daddy, Tony Trilling whispered in my ear, "Thank you, Cher," and gave me this awesome kiss.

We were in my room, cramming for a pop quiz in algebra when Amber ran in with a stack of periodicals. "Did you see this?" she asked, hurling 'zines like Frisbees through the air.

"You're late," Janet said. "We're like done with sines and cosines."

"How tragic," Amber snapped. "Not that I missed your little math review, but that you'd think I'd care."

"Cher!" De screeched. "We made *People* magazine. It's the pics of us with Tony in the clubhouse at camp! He's wearing his cap and gown. They got you right at the moment of smooch. Oh, girl, you look so cute. And look, that hand raised behind you, that's me. That's my hand."

But I was looking at the supermarket tabloid the fashion calamity had tossed onto my bed. There on the front page was a fuzzy black-and-white photo of two people caught in a private lip-locked moment. I definitely recognized the couple.

"And speaking of tragic." Amber turned to me. "Check out that headline. Painful, isn't it? To think Tony Trilling could be so deceiving."

The headline said, " 'Exclusive. Tony's poolside playmate. Teen tennis star's mystery lady. More inside.' "

I rifled through the colorful pages of three-hundred-pound pigs and slightly slimmer alien abduction victims to the center spread. It featured six smaller but equally fuzzy photos of Tony and me. "He was cheating on you," Amber announced dramatically.

De scrambled across the bed to peer over my shoulder. "Well, at least the mystery woman's wearing a decent chemise." She grinned. "A little lace confection by Versace, I believe."

"Major snaps, girlfriend. You totally identified the brand," I said.

"How can you people think of fashion at a time like this?" Amber was stunned. "When I flashed those pics at Harrison, he was horrified. He urged me not to show them to you. Maybe he was right. I seem to care more about Tony's embarrassing betrayal than you do."

I couldn't help glancing at the postcard propped against the antique brass lamp on my French provincial bedside table. The card had arrived yesterday. On one side, under a banner that read Greetings from Australia, there was a photo of surfers riding this monster wave. On the other was Tony's note. "I'd say 'Wish you were here,' but you are. You're in my thoughts and heart, Cher. Thanks for an unforgettable graduation day." I smiled, then realized what Amber was saying. "Harry was being protective of me?" I marveled.

"Josh's influence," De guessed.

"In fact, Harrison and I got into the worst fight over this issue." Amber threw herself onto my bed and lay there, snuffling into my pink Laura Ashley duvet cover. Then she flung herself onto her back. "So now, like you, Cher," she said emotionally, "I'm wounded and alone."

"We're young, Amber," I reminded her. "We have our whole lives ahead. Right now there are more important things in life for us than pair bonding and snaring a boo."

"Yeah, like school and science and math," Janet pointed out.

We all turned to her, dumbfounded. "Er, not exactly, Janet," De said.

"And shopping," the brainer ventured.

"Yesss!" we screamed.

"CPK beats CPR for resuscitation anytime," I said.

"To the Beverly Center," De proposed.

And slipping into our Nine Wests, Joan & Davids, and Capezio pumps, we grabbed our Escada totes and Vuitton epi leather purses, slung Anna Sui and Isaac Mizrahi sweaters over our Calvins and Laurens, and prepared to ease our faux broken hearts at the mall.

About the Author

H. B. Gilmour is the author of the bestselling
novelizations *Clueless* and *Pretty in Pink,* as well as
*Clueless™: Cher's Guide to . . . Whatever, Clue-
less™: Achieving Personal Perfection, Clueless™:
Friend or Faux, Clueless™: Baldwin from Another
Planet, Clueless™: Cher and Cher Alike, Clarissa
Explains It All: Boys,* the well-reviewed young-
adult novel *Ask Me If I Care,* and more than fifteen
other books for adults and young people.

What's it like to be a Witch?

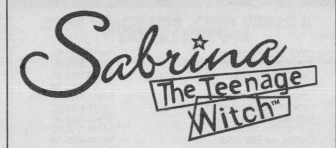

Sabrina The Teenage Witch™

"I'm 16, I'm a witch, and I *still* have to go to school?"

◆◆◆◆◆

#1 Sabrina, the Teenage Witch
by David Cody Weiss and Bobbi JG Weiss

#2 Showdown at the Mall
by Diana G. Gallagher

#3 Good Switch, Bad Switch
by David Cody Weiss and Bobbi JG Weiss

#4 Halloween Havoc
by Diana Gallagher

Based on the hit TV series

Look for a new title every other month.

From Archway Paperbacks
Published by Pocket Books

1345-03